He moved closer.

She could feel the warmth of his body, and the wild longings it produced tricked her into looking up. His eyes trapped hers. His free hand moved to her face and lightly touched her mouth. The slight sensation made her tremble.

"Stop that," he said. "You're no more an experienced woman than I am a monk. I've had women. And if you're not damned careful, I'll have you."

"After I've been embalmed, maybe," she retorted. "And will you please remember that I'm engaged to Al?" she said too quickly.

His fingers were under her chin, sensually tracing the long line of her throat, and she could taste his smoky breath on her lips, feel the strength, warmth and power of his lean body and smell his cologne and faint leathery scent.

"Sure you are. For now."

DIANA PALMER

After the Music

MIRA®

ISBN 1-55166-452-6

AFTER THE MUSIC

Printed in U.S.A.

To Hope and Lamar

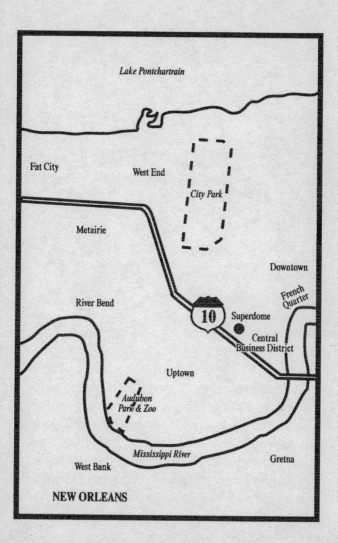

Lake Pontchartrain

Fat City

West End

City Park

Metairie

Downtown

River Bend

French
Quarter

10 Superdome

Central
Business District

Uptown

Audubon
Park & Zoo

Mississippi River

West Bank

Gretna

NEW ORLEANS

Chapter One

It was sad to see a tour end, Sabina Cane thought as she watched the electricians strike the lights at the auditorium where she and the band had performed the night before. It had been a sellout performance here in Savannah, and thank God for road tours. Times had been hard lately, and as it was, they'd make only a small profit after all the hands were paid. Sabina often wondered if there would ever come a time when she'd have financial security. Then she threw back her head and laughed at her own silly fears. She was doing what she loved best, after all. Without singing, she'd have no life at all, so she ought to be grateful that she had work. Besides, she and The Bricks and Sand Band were already booked for two weeks back home in New Orleans at one of the best clubs in town. And this month on the road had netted them some invaluable publicity.

She stared down the deserted, littered aisles, and spared a sympathetic smile for the tired men taking down equipment at this hour of the night. They had to be in New Orleans tomorrow for rehearsals, so there was no time to waste.

Sabina stretched lazily. Her slender body in its satin shorts and sequined camisole top and thigh-high cuffed pirate's boots was deliciously outlined by the fabric that was her trademark. The Satin Girl had wavy dark hair, which she wore down to her waist, and eyes almost like silver. Her complexion had been likened to pure pearl, and she had eyelashes no photographer believed were actually real.

Albert Thorndon grinned at her from the front of the auditorium, where he was passing the time with her road manager, Dennis Hart, who was also doubling as their booking agent. Dennis had done well so far for a young publicist seeking new directions. She smiled at both of them, waving at Al.

He was one of her best friends. She'd met him through her childhood pal, Jessica, who was hopelessly in love with Al. He was Jess's boss at Thorn Oil. Al didn't know about that infatuation, and Sabina had never betrayed Jess by telling him. The three of them went around together infrequently, and maybe at the very beginning Al had been mildly attracted to her. But Sabina wanted nothing from a man in any emotional or physical sense, and she let him know it right off the bat. After that, he'd accepted her as a friend. It was Al who'd managed to get them the club engagement in New Orleans, and he'd flown here all the way from Louisiana to tell her so. Thorn Oil had many subsidiaries. One of them was that nightclub in New Orleans. She wondered if his older brother knew what Al had done.

She'd heard plenty about Hamilton Regan Thorndon the Third, and most of it was unfavorable. The elder brother was the head honcho of Thorn Oil, which was headquartered in New Orleans, and he had a reputation for more than a shrewd business head. Rumor had it that he went through women relentlessly, leaving a trail of broken hearts behind him. He was the kind of man Sabina hated on sight, and she was glad Al had never tried to introduce her to his family. There wasn't much family, apparently. Only the two brothers and their widowed mother, who was on the stage somehow or other and spent most of her time in Europe. Al didn't talk about his family much.

At times, it all seemed odd to her. Al was always avoiding his family. He never even invited Jessica to those big company barbecues out at the family ranch in Beaumont, Texas, and Jess had been his secretary for two years. Sabina found his behavior fascinating, but she never questioned him about it. She'd thought at first that her background might have been the reason that he didn't introduce her, and she'd felt murderous. But when she realized that he'd left Jessica off the guest list, too, she calmed down. Anyway, Al didn't know about her past. Only Jess did, and Jess was a clam.

Al murmured something else to Dennis, and with a wave of his hand, went to join Sabina. His green eyes frankly approved of the baby-blue and silver-satin shorts that displayed her long, tanned legs to advantage. She laughed at the stage leer, knowing it was only an old joke between them.

"Well, aren't you the picture, Satin Girl?" he said with a laugh. He had dark hair and was just her height.

"I don't know. Am I?" She struck a pose.

"My kingdom for a camera," he sighed. "Where do you get those sexy costumes, anyway?"

"I make them," she confided, and laughed at his astonished reassessment of her garments. "Well, I did take a sewing course, and it relaxes me when I'm not singing."

"Little Miss Domestic," he teased.

"Not me, mister," she drawled. "I know all I care to about housework."

"In that tiny apartment," he sighed. "Don't make me laugh. You could mop the floor with a paper towel."

"It's home," she said defensively.

"It would be better stocked if you wouldn't give away everything you earn," he said, glaring at her. "Secondhand furniture, secondhand TV, secondhand everything, just because you're the softest touch going. No wonder you never have any money!''

"A lot of my neighbors are worse off than I am," she reminded him. "If you don't believe in poverty, let me introduce you around my neighborhood. You'll get an education in the desperation of inescapable struggle."

"I know, you don't have to rub it in." He stuck his hands in his pockets. "I just wish you'd save a bit."

"I save some." She shrugged.

"End of conversation," he murmured dryly. "I know when I'm beaten. Are you coming to my party tomorrow night?"

"What party?"

"The one I'm giving at my apartment."

She'd never known Al to give a party. She stared at him suspiciously. "Who's going to be there?"

"A lot of people you don't know, including Thorn."

Just the sound of his nickname threw her. "Hamilton Regan Thorndon the Third in the flesh?" she taunted.

"If you call him that, do it from the other side of a door, will you?" he cautioned, smiling. "He hates it. I've called him Thorn since we were kids."

"I suppose he's a stuffy old businessman with a thick paunch and a bald head?"

"He's thirty-four," he told her. His eyes were calculating. "Why do you react that way every time I mention him? You clam up."

She stared down at her black boots. "He uses women."

"Well, of course he does," he burst out. "For God's sake, they use him, too! He's rich and he doesn't mind spending money on them. He's a bachelor."

Her mind drifted to the past. Rich men with money. Bait. Using it like bait. Catching desperate women. She winced at the memory. "Mama," she whispered and tears welled up. She turned away, shaking with subdued rage.

"Odd that he isn't married."

Al was watching her with open curiosity. "My God, no one could live with Thorn." He laughed bitterly. "Why do you think our mother stays in Europe, and I have an apartment in the city?"

"You said he loves women," she reminded him.

"Nobody is allowed that close," he said flatly. "Thorn was betrayed once, and he's never cared about a woman since, except in the obvious ways. Thorn is like his nickname. He's prickly and passionate and rock stubborn. His executives bring jugs of Maalox to board meetings."

"I'd bring a battle-ax," she commented dryly. "Or maybe a bazooka. I don't like arrogant ladies' men."

"Yes, I know. You two would hit it off like thunder," he returned, "because Thorn doesn't like aggressive women. He prefers the curling kitten type."

She'd have bet he'd been hoping all his life for someone to match him. She was almost sorry because the pattern of her own life had made it impossible for her to be interested. It would have been fascinating to take him on. But she was as cold as the leather of the boots she wore onstage. Ironic. She was a rock star with a sensuous reputation, and her experience of men had been limited to a chaste kiss here and there. She found men unsatisfying and unreliable. Her heart was whole. She'd never given it. She never would.

She got up from her perch and flexed her shoulders wearily. It had been a long night.

"I could use a few hours' sleep," she said on a sigh. "Thanks for coming all this way to give us the news."

"My pleasure," he said. "The vocalist who had been hired by the club manager was involved in a car crash. She'll be okay, but she won't perform for a while. They were relieved that you and the band didn't mind rushing home to fill the spot."

Sabina smiled. "We're always rushing somewhere. We're grateful to get the work."

"About tomorrow night." He seemed oddly hesitant.

"The party?" She studied him and sensed something. "You're up to something. What is it?"

He shook his head ruefully. "You read me too well. There's this benefit."

"Aha!"

"I'll tell you more about it tomorrow night when I pick you up. I need some help. It's for underprivileged kids," he added.

"Then count me in, whatever it is." She stifled a yawn. "Who's the hostess for you?"

"Jessica." He looked sad and lost. His eyes met hers and fell. "I wish...nothing."

"You've never invited Jess to a party before," she remarked gently.

"Thorn would eat her alive if he thought I was interested in her," he said, grinding his teeth. "I told him I couldn't get anyone else to hostess.... Oh, hell, I've got to run. My pilot's waiting at the airport. I didn't have anything better to do, so I thought I'd catch your last performance and tell you about the club date. Pick you up tomorrow night at six, okay?"

"Okay," she said, reluctant to let the matter drop. What a horror his brother sounded! "See you. And thanks for the club date, pal."

"My pleasure. Night." He turned and walked away, and her eyes followed him with open speculation. Could he be getting interested in Jessica? What a wonderful thing that would be. Her two best friends. She smiled to herself.

It was late afternoon when Sabina finally got to her own apartment. She walked up the steps, gazing fondly down at the block of row houses. She'd lived here all her adult life, ever since she'd left the orphanage at the age of eighteen. It wasn't a socially acceptable neighborhood. It was a poor one. But she had good neighbors and good friends here, and she loved the children who played on the cracked sidewalk. It was close to the bay, so she could hear the ships as they came into port, and she could smell the sea breezes. From her room on the fourth floor, she sometimes watched them as they passed, the heaving old freighters moving with an odd grace. But the very best thing about her apartment was the rent. She could afford it.

"Back home, I see, Miss Cane," Mr. Rafferty said at the foot of the staircase. He was about seventy and bald and always wore an undershirt and trousers around the building. He lived on his Social Security checks and had no family—unless you counted the other tenants.

"Yes, sir." Sabina grinned. "Got something for you," she murmured. She dug into her bag and produced a small sack of pralines she'd bought on the way home. "For your sweet tooth," she said, handing them over.

"Pralines." Mr. Rafferty sighed. He took a bite, savoring the taste. "My favorite! Miss

Cane, you're always bringing me things.'' He shook his head, staring with sad eyes. "And I have nothing to give you.''

"You're my friend,'' she said. "And besides, I've already got everything I need.''

"You give it all away,'' he uttered darkly. "How will you heat your place with winter coming on?''

"I'll burn the furniture,'' she said in a stage whisper, and was rewarded with a faint smile from the pugnacious, proud old man who never smiled for any of the other tenants. He was disliked by everyone, except Sabina, who saw through the gruff exterior to the frightened, lonely man underneath. "See you!'' Laughing, she bounded upstairs in her jeans and tank top, and Mr. Rafferty clutched his precious pralines and ambled back into his room.

Billy and Bess, the blond twins who lived next door, laughed when they saw her coming. "Miss Dean said you'd be back today!'' they chattered, naming the landlady. "Did you have a big crowd?''

"Just right,'' she told them, extracting two of the huge lollipops she'd bought along with the pralines. "Here. Don't eat them before your dinner or your mama'll skin me!"

"Thanks!" they said in unison, eyeing the candy with adoration.

"Now I really have to get some sleep," she told them. "We've got a gig downtown!"

"Really?" Billy asked, wide-eyed. He and his sister were ten, and Sabina's profession awed them. Imagine, a rock star in their own building! The other kids down the block were green with envy.

"Really. So keep the noise down, huh?" she added in a conspiratorial whisper.

"You bet! We'll be your lookouts," Bess seconded.

She blew them a kiss and went inside. The twins' only parent was an alcoholic mother who loved them, but was hardly reliable. Sabina tried to look out for them at night, taking them into her apartment to sleep if Matilda stayed out, as she often did. Social workers came and went, but they couldn't produce any antidote for the hopeless poverty Matilda lived in, and threats to take the children away only produced tears and promises of immediate sobriety. Unfortunately, Matilda's promise lasted about an hour or two, or until the social worker left, whichever came first.

Sabina knew that kind of hopelessness first-hand. Until her mother died and she was put in the orphanage, she'd often gone hungry and cold herself. Losing her mother in the brutal way she did hadn't helped. But the struggle had given her a fixation about rich men and hard living. She hated both. With the voice that God had given her, she was determined to claw her way out of poverty and make something of her life. She was doing it, too. If only it had been in time to save her mother...

She lay down on the bed with a sigh and closed her eyes. She was so tired. She put everything she had, everything she was, into her performances. When they were over, she collapsed. Dead tired. Sometimes she felt alive only in front of an audience, feeding on their adrenaline, the loud clapping and the cheers as she belted out the songs in her clear, haunting voice. Her own feet would echo the rhythms, and her body would sway. Her long, dark hair would fly and her silver-blue eyes would snap and sparkle with the electricity of her perform-ances. She withheld nothing, but it was telling on her. All the long nights were wearing her down, and she was losing weight. But she had to keep going. She couldn't afford to slow down now, when she and the band were so close to the golden ring. They were drawing bigger crowds all the time wherever they appeared, and getting great coverage in the local press. Someday they'd get a recording contract, and then, look out!

Smiling as she daydreamed about that, she closed her eyes and felt the lumpy mattress under her with a wistful sigh. Just a few minutes rest would do it. Just a few minutes...

The loud pounding on the door woke her up. Drowsily, she got to her feet and opened it, to find Al on the other side.

"I fell asleep," Sabina explained. "What time is it?"

"Six o'clock. Hurry and throw something on. You'll feel better when you've eaten."

"What are you feeding me?" she asked on a yawn, preceding him into the apartment.

"Chicken Kiev," he told her. "Pommes de terre, and broccoli in hollandaise sauce—with cherries jubilee for dessert."

"You must have kept Susi in the kitchen all day!" she exclaimed with a laugh, picturing Al's cook, a stooped little Cajun woman cursing a blue streak as she prepared that luscious repast.

"I did," he said, green eyes gleaming. "I had to promise her a bonus, too."

"Well, she certainly deserves it. Make yourself comfortable. I'll be out in a jiffy." She took a quick shower and pulled on an elegant electric-blue satin dress with spaghetti straps, a square neckline, and a drop waist with a semi-full skirt. It suited her slenderness and gave her gray eyes a blue look. Normally she'd never have been able to afford it on her budget, but she'd found it at an elegant used dress shop and paid only a fraction of its original price. Bargain hunting was one of her specialties. It had to be, on her erratic salary. She wore black sling pumps with it, and carried a dainty little black evening bag, and put on the long cashmere coat, because nights were getting cold in late autumn. She left her hair long instead of putting it into a high French twist, as she usually did in the evening. When she went back

out into the living room, Al got to his feet and
sighed.

"You dish," he murmured. "What an eye-
catcher!"

"Why does that make you look so smug?"
she asked suspiciously.

"I told you I had a project in mind," he said
after a minute. "You remember hearing me
talk about the children's hospital I'm trying to
get funds to build?"

"Yes," she said, waiting.

"I'm trying to put together a benefit for it.
On local television. If I had a couple of sponsors, and you for a drawing card, I could get
some local talent and present it to the local stations." He grinned. "I guarantee we'd raise
more than enough."

"You know I'd do it for you, without pay,"
she said. "But we're not big enough..."

"Yes, you are," he said stubbornly. "A television appearance here would give you some
great publicity. Look, I'm not asking you to do
it for that reason and you know it, so don't
ruffle up at me. The kids will benefit most, and
I've got some other talent lined up as well,"
he told her. "But I can't sell the idea to the

television stations until I've got the sponsors. I want to wheedle Thorn into being one of them.''

''Will he?''

''If he's persuaded,'' he said, with a sly glance at her.

''Now, wait a minute,'' she said curtly. ''I am not playing up to your poisonous brother, for any reason.''

''You don't have to play up to him. Just be friendly. Be yourself.''

She frowned. ''You aren't going to paint me into a corner, are you?''

''Scout's honor,'' he promised with a flash of white teeth. ''Trust me.''

''I don't trust anybody, even you,'' she said with a smile.

''I'm working on that. Let's go.''

He led her down the long flight of stairs.

''Couldn't you ask him yourself?'' she murmured. ''After all, blood is thicker...''

''Thorn's kind of miffed with me.''

''Why?''

Al stuck his hands in his pockets with a sigh and glanced at her ruefully. ''He brought a girl home for me last night.''

Her eyes widened. "He what?"

"Brought a girl home for me. A very nice girl, with excellent connections, whose father owns an oil refinery. He was giving a dinner party, you see."

"My God!" she burst out.

"I called my mother after it was over, and she called up and chewed on his ear for a while. That made him mad. He doesn't like her very much most of the time, and he needs that refinery damned bad." He shrugged. "If I could get him a refinery, he'd sure rush over to sponsor my benefit."

"You could buy him one," she suggested.

"With what? I'm broke. Not totally, but I don't have the kind of capital I'd need for business on that scale. I'm a partner on paper only, until I come into my share of Dad's estate next year."

"I'm beginning to get a very interesting picture of Hamilton Regan Thorndon the Third," she said stiffly. "A matchmaker, is he?"

"That's about the size of it," Al confessed. He gestured toward his car when they reached the street. "I'm parked over there."

She followed him, scowling. "Does he do this to you often?"

"Only when he needs something he can't buy." He sighed. "You'd never guess how many businessmen have eligible daughters they want to marry off. Especially businessmen with refineries and blocks of oil stock and..."

"But that's inhuman!"

"So is Thorn, from time to time." He unlocked the car and helped her inside. "Haven't you wondered why I usually keep you and Jessica away from company parties?"

"I'm beginning to realize," she said to herself. She waited until he got inside the green Mercedes-Benz and started the engine before she added, "He doesn't want you associating with the peons, I gather?"

He stiffened, started to deny it, and then huffed miserably. "He's not marriage-minded himself. Thorn Oil is worth millions, with all its subsidiaries. He wants an heir for it. But with just the right girl, you see. Jessica has been married before, and her family isn't socially prominent," he said, biting it out. "Thorn would savage her."

It all became crystal clear. Everything...how

he felt about Jessica, why he'd been so secretive. "Oh, Al," she breathed piteously. "Oh, Al, how horrible for you!"

"Next year I can fight him," he said. "When I've got money of my own. But for now I have to lie low and bide my time."

"I'd punch him out," she growled softly, gray eyes throwing off silver sparks, her long hair swirling like silk as her head jerked.

He glanced at her as he drove toward his apartment down the brightly lit streets. "Yes, I believe you would. You're like him. Fire and high temper and impulsive actions." He smiled. "You'd be a match, even for my brother."

"With all due respect, I don't want your brother."

"Yes, I know. But please don't take a swing at him tonight. I need you."

"Now, wait a minute…"

"Just to help present my case, nothing else," he promised. His smile faded as he studied her. "I wouldn't strand you with him. Thorn isn't much good with innocents. You'll know what I mean when you see the woman he's got with him tonight. She's as much a bar-

racuda as he is. I only want you to help me
convince him to sponsor the benefit. I'll get an
accompanist and you can do the aria from Ma-
dame Butterfly for him.''

"He likes opera?" she asked.

"He loves it."

She eyed him closely. "How does he feel
about rock singers?"

He shifted restlessly, and looked worried.
"Well..."

"How?"

His jaw clenched. "Actually, he's never
said. Don't worry, we'll find out together."

She had grave misgivings, but she didn't say
anything. After all, his older brother would
probably be nothing like she imagined. He
might like women, but she pictured him as a
retiring sort of man like the pictures of businessmen she'd seen in magazines. She knew
all too well that a rich man didn't have to be
good-looking to get women.

Al's house overlooked the bay, and Sabina
dearly loved it. It was white and stately, and
had once belonged to his grandmother. She
could picture the huge living room being the
scene of elegant balls in the early days of New

Orleans. There were shrubs all around it, assorted camellias and gardenia and jasmine. Now, of course, everything was dormant, but Sabina could imagine the grounds bursting with color, as they would in the spring.

Jessica came darting out of the big living room, where several people were socializing over drinks, and her face was as red as her hair. She was small and sweet, and Sabina loved her. She and Jess went back a long way. They'd shared some good times when Sabina was at the orphanage just around the corner from where Jessica lived. They'd met by accident, but a firm friendship had developed, and lasted all these years.

"Hi, Sabina!" Jessica said quickly, then turned immediately to Al. "We're in trouble. You invited Beck Henton."

"Yes. So?" Al asked blankly.

"Well, he and Thorn are competing for that oil refinery in Houston. Had you forgotten?"

Al slapped his forehead. "Damn!"

"Anyway, they just went out the back door together, and Thorn was squinting one eye. You know what that means."

"Damn!" Al repeated. "I was going to ask

Beck to help sponsor my benefit,'' he growled. ''Well, that's blown it. I'd better go and try to save him.''

Sabina stared after him with wide, curious eyes. She was getting a strange picture of the sedate older brother.

''I'd better get Beck's chauffeur,'' Jessica said miserably. ''He'll be needed.''

''Before you go, is there any ginger ale in there?'' she asked, nodding toward the bar in the living room.

''Not a drop. But I left you a bottle in the kitchen. I'll see you in a minute.''

''Thanks!'' Sabina darted quickly into the kitchen and filled a glass with ice. She was just reaching for the bottle of ginger ale when the back door suddenly flung open and, just as quickly, slammed again.

She turned, and froze in place when she saw him. He was tall and slender, with the kind of body that reminded Sabina of the men who appear in television commercials. He was powerful for all that slenderness, and the darkness of his tuxedo emphasized his jet black hair and the deep tan of his face and hands. His eyes were surrounded by thick, black lashes, and they glittered at her.

"Hand me a cup of that," he said in a crisp voice, holding out a lean, long-fingered hand. There was no jewelry on it, but she got a glimpse of crisp black hair on his wrist surrounding a Rolex watch.

She handed him the ice automatically, noting a faint scar on his cheek, near his eye. His nose was arrow-straight and gave him a look of arrogance. He had a jutting jaw that hinted of stubbornness, and his mouth was perfect, the most masculine mouth she'd ever seen. He was fascinating, and she couldn't take her eyes off him.

"What's so fascinating, honey?" he drawled. "Haven't you ever seen a man with a black eye before?"

This, she thought, must be the Beck Henton they'd discussed, because he certainly didn't fit the long, pretentious name Al's brother had.

"Not many walking around in tuxedos." She grinned. He did fascinate her, not only with the way he looked, but with that air of authority that embodied him.

She seemed to fascinate him, too, because a

smile played at the corners of his mouth as he wrapped the ice in a tea towel and held it just under his bruised eye. He moved closer, and she saw that the glittering eyes under the jutting brow were a pale, icy-blue. The color was shocking in so dark a face.

He let his gaze fall to her smooth, faintly tanned shoulders and down the bodice of the trendy dress to her long, slender legs encased in blue-patterned stockings. They moved back up slowly, past her long neck and over the delicate planes of her face to her soft mouth, her high cheekbones, her dark, wavy hair and to the incredibly long lashes over her silver eyes.

"Why are you hiding in here?" he asked, breaking the silence.

"I came for some ginger ale," she confessed, showing the bottle. "I don't drink, you see. Jessica hides some soft drinks for me, so I don't have to look repressed in front of Al's guests."

He cocked his head. "You don't look repressed." That faint smile was still playing on his firm mouth. "Al's secretary must be a friend of yours?"

"A very good one."

"Jessica's all right. Al said he couldn't get anyone else to hostess for him, and she's doing a pretty good job."

Faint praise, she thought, and a bit condescending, but he had a right to his opinion. "You're going to have a gorgeous shiner, there," she remarked.

"You ought to see the other guy," he mused.

She sighed. "Poor Hamilton Regan Thorndon the Third. I hope you didn't hit him too hard."

His dark eyebrows arched, and his eyes widened. "Poor Hamilton...?"

"Al said the two of you were competing for an oil refinery," she volunteered, grinning impishly. "Why don't you just leave the oil in the ground and pump out what you need a little at a time?"

He chuckled softly. "You're impertinent, miss."

"Why thank you, Mr. Henton. You are Beck Henton, aren't you?" she persisted. "You certainly couldn't be Al's brother. You don't look like a man with a mile long name."

"I don't? And what do you imagine Al's brother looks like?"

"Dark and chubby and slightly graying," she said, fascinated by his faint smile.

"My God, I never knew Al to lie."

"But he didn't. I mean, he didn't ever describe his brother." She poured ginger ale into her glass, lifted it up and peeked at him over its rim. "You really shouldn't have hit Al's brother. Now he'll leave and I won't get a shot at him."

One eye narrowed. "Why did you want to?"

"Well, he's got an oil company," she said. "And there's a project..."

Before she could tell him why, his expression grew stern and he laughed unpleasantly. "There's always a project." He moved closer. "Why don't you have a shot at me, honey? I've got an oil company myself."

"Aren't you...with someone?" she asked nervously. He was so close that she could feel the vibrant energy of him, smell his expensive cologne. He towered over her.

"I'm always with someone," he murmured, letting his fingers toy with strands of her soft hair. "Not that it matters. They all look alike, eventually."

"Mr. Henton…" she began, trying to move away.

He backed her against the counter and pinned her there with the delicate, controlled weight of his body. He was almost touching her, but not quite. Her hands shook as he took the glass from her and set it aside on the counter.

"Shhh," he said softly, touching her mouth with one long finger. He wasn't smiling now. His eyes were darkening, intense. He tossed the towel and ice aside, and framed her oval face in his big, warm hands. They felt callused, as if he used them in hard work, and she felt threatened.

"You mustn't…"

"We're cutting a corner or two, that's all," he whispered, bending. "You're very lovely."

She should move, she should push away! But her hands flattened helplessly on his shirt-front, and she felt hard muscle and warmth against her cold fingers. His breath teased her lips as he poised his mouth over hers.

"No," she protested weakly and tried to move away.

His hips pressed her into the counter, and the twisting motion of her body provoked a shocking reaction. He drew in a sharp breath, and his fingers tightened on her face. "My God, it's been years since that's happened so quickly with a woman," he said curtly and then his mouth was on hers.

She stiffened, feeling the shock from her head to her toes, which tried to curl up in her high heels as his lips relented. He seemed to feel her uneasiness, her reticence. He drew away and searched her face with odd, puzzled eyes. Then, slowly he lowered his head again and traced her bottom lip with his teeth, slowly, gently in masterful exploration that was years beyond her experience of men. Her fingers clung to the lapels of his jacket and her breath came quickly. She could taste him, the smoky and minty warmth of his mouth doing wild things to her pulse.

"Yes, like that," he whispered into her slowly parting lips. "A little more, honey...yes. Kiss me back this time. Kiss me..."

He incited her in wild, reckless ways. It was like some wild fantasy, that she could be standing in an intimate embrace, kissing a man whom she'd only just met in a deserted kitchen. He was no ordinary man, either; he was an expert at this; he knew ways of using his mouth that she'd never even imagined.

She gasped as his tongue probed and his mouth demanded. All at once the hunger broke through her natural reserve and she felt warmth spread through her body. A tiny, surprising moan broke from her lips as she went up on tiptoe and gave him her mouth hungrily. Her hands reached up to the thick, cool waves of his hair and she held his head to hers.

"God!" he groaned. His arms lifted her and the room seemed to whirl away. It was the wildest, deepest, hungriest kiss she'd ever shared with a man, and it didn't seem as if he had any intention of stopping. She should be fighting him. Why couldn't she fight?

A long minute later, he set her back on her feet and looked down into her wide gray eyes with curiosity and caution. One of his blue eyes narrowed, and a warning bell rang somewhere in her mind, but her body was throbbing wildly and she hardly connected the telltale sign.

"You're gifted, lady," he breathed, studying her. "Not very experienced yet, but I can take care of that. Come home with me."

Her face burned and her lips trembled. "I can't," she whispered shakily.

"Why not?" His eyes blazed down at her body.

"I...what about Al?" she began.

He made a rough sound under his breath. "What about him, for God's sake? Have you got some wild crush on him? You won't get to first base, I promise you. Al's bringing that damned rock singer he's courting. I came because of her, but I can deal with her later." He touched her cheek gently and seemed oddly hesitant, mistaking her frozen posture for fear instead of the shock it really was. "I won't hurt you," he said mildly. "I won't rush you, either. We can discuss...projects."

The words began to take affect on her numb brain, and she stared up at him with dawning comprehension.

"Rock singer?"

He looked utterly dangerous, the tender

lover suddenly growing cold and businesslike and threatening. "Al's got himself a new girl. But not for long," he added on a short laugh. "That's got nothing to do with you and me. You said you need money; let's go talk about it."

"You're...Hamilton Regan Thorndon the Third," she said.

He cocked an eyebrow. "Smart lady. Does it make a difference? I told you I had an oil company. Come on, honey, let's get away from this crowd." He touched her shoulder, lazily, caressingly. "You won't go away empty-handed, I promise."

She felt sick all over—sick that she'd let him kiss her, that she'd responded. She felt as her mother must have years ago, but with one major difference: she wasn't desperate. She'd never be desperate enough, and her kindling eyes told him so. She began to tremble with the force of her anger, her disgust.

"Hey, what is it?" he asked suddenly, frowning.

"You have such a line, Mr. Thorndon the Third," she said with a voice as cold as ice. Her fists were clenched at her sides as she backed sharply away from him. "'You won't go away empty-handed,'" she mimicked.

"How suddenly principled you are, lady," he said bitterly. "You're the one who started talking terms right off the bat. Okay, I'm willing. How much?"

Oh, Lord, what a mess she'd made of things. Why hadn't she said something about the project? Now he thought she was a prostitute! But what a monumental ego he had, she thought, glaring up at him. "You couldn't afford me," she told him.

His eyes ran over her body again and this time there was no appreciation in his stare. "You overestimate yourself. I'd say twenty dollars would do it."

She slapped him. It was completely unpremeditated, without thought, but she wasn't taking any more insults from this creature, even if he was Al's brother.

He didn't even flinch. His cheek turned red, but he simply stared at her with those icy eyes.

"You'll pay for that," he said quietly.

"Make me," she challenged, backing away. "Come on, oil baron, hit me back." She was beautiful in her fury, silver eyes flashing, black hair flying, body taut and poised and elegant. "I'm not afraid of you."

His face gave nothing away; his gaze was unblinking and hard. "Who are you?" he asked sternly.

"I'm the tooth fairy," she said with a mocking smile. "Too bad you didn't lose any to Mr. Henton; I've got a pocket full of quarters."

She turned, forgetting her ginger ale, and strode out the door and through the house. She was livid by the time she reached the crowded living room.

Al spotted her, moving forward with a glass in his hand. He looked worried and nervous, but when he saw Sabina's face he looked shocked.

"What happened?"

"Never mind." She would hate to tell him. "Where's Mr. Henton?"

"Gone home in a snit, with a broken nose," he grumbled. "So much for that potential sponsor." He sighed. "Well, we'll just have to work on Thorn."

"Al, about working on your brother..."

A door slammed, and even amid the noise of the guests, she knew who it was and why.

She stiffened as Al looked over her shoulder and grinned.

"Well, Beck sure left you a present, didn't he?" Al chuckled. "Why didn't you duck?"

"I did," came a familiar, cold drawl from behind her. "Are you going to introduce me?" he asked, pretending ignorance.

"Sure." Al placed a casual arm across Sabina's shoulder and turned her to face the man with the black eye. Al sounded casual, but his arm was tense and trembling a little. "This is Sabina Cane."

The tall man looked suddenly murderous. "The rock singer?"

"Yes," Al said defensively.

The man who'd kissed her so passionately not five minutes before glared at Sabina as if he'd like to cut her throat.

"I should have known," he said with a harsh laugh, ramming one lean hand into his pants pocket. "You look the part."

She curtsied sweetly. "Thank you, Mr. Thorndon the Third."

Al glanced from one to the other with open curiosity. "Thorn, there's something I want to talk to you about," he said.

"Forget it," Thorn told him. He gave Sabina a long, insulting appraisal. "Your taste in women stinks." He turned and walked straight toward an elegant blonde in a gold lamé body-suit. The woman slipped into his arms, clinging to him like glue.

Sabina glared at him with eyes that burned when she saw him bend to kiss the blonde warmly on the mouth. She averted her gaze. "Al, I can't stay here. I can't possibly."

"Sabina, I'm sorry…"

She spotted Jessica and motioned to her. "Can you run me home?"

"Sure, what's wrong?"

"I just have a bad headache, Al." Sabina lied smoothly. She couldn't go into it now. "I'm sorry, I thought it would get better."

"If it's because of Thorn," he began, glaring at his brother, "I apologize for his bad manners."

"I'd like to tell him what to do with them, too," she told Al. "But my head's splitting. Jessica?"

"I'm ready. Come on. See you later, boss," she told Al with a shy smile.

"I'll talk to Thorn," Al said brusquely.

"Don't waste your breath on him," Sabina added. "Good night."

She walked out the door with a breathless Jessica right behind, grateful for the nippy autumn air and the dark.

"What happened in the kitchen?" Jessica demanded as they were driving back toward Sabina's apartment.

"I antagonized him," Sabina said stiffly. "Al will never forgive me, but I couldn't stand that man another minute!"

"Al says that Thorn is used to expecting the worst and he usually finds it. He's a sad kind of man, really. He doesn't let anybody get close; he spends most of his time all alone."

"Alone?" Sabina said gruffly. "That's not what I saw...."

"Window dressing," Jessica replied as she sped down the street where her friend lived. "His women come and go. Mostly they go."

"How do you know so much about him?" Sabina asked.

"He comes in and out of our office. His own offices are in the new building, the addition. But he and Al have business dealings they have to discuss now and then. He's always polite.

Once, he even brought me coffee when I was hurrying to get some correspondence out for him and Al,'' she added with a smile.

He could afford to be polite to Al's secretary, Sabina thought angrily. But if Al got serious about Jessica, she knew Thorn would wage a desperate battle. He had said as much with that offhand remark at the party. And Al did feel something for Jess, Sabina was sure of it. She wanted so much to tell Jessica what she suspected.

''Thorn probably bribes people when he can't get them any other way,'' Sabina grumbled.

Jessica pulled into a parking space outside the apartment building and glanced at her friend. ''I'll bet he's never needed a bribe,'' she sighed. ''But Al's terrified of him, you know? So am I, really. If I ever looked twice at Al, I'll bet Thorn would have me transferred to Saudi Arabia or somewhere.''

Yes, Sabina thought miserably, being nice to Al's secretary was one thing. But Hamilton Regan Thorndon the Third would cut Jess up like sausage for merely smiling at his brother.

''Just remember one thing. Al isn't blind

about you," Sabina said softly. "And if he cared enough, he'd even take on big brother."

"He'd only notice me if I died and there was nobody to make coffee," Jess groaned.

"Ha! Well, I guess I'll go up and eat some toast. Damn Hamilton Regan Thorndon the Third, anyway," she muttered. "He's cost me my supper. Imagine having to work for him!"

"His secretaries kind of come and go, like his women," Jessica confided. "He's hard on women. They say he hates them."

Sabina felt herself shudder. "Yes, I felt that. He's very cold."

"Not in bed, I'll bet," Jessica said under her breath.

Sabina's face flushed, and she got out before Jess could see it. "Thanks for the ride! Want to have lunch one day?"

"I'll call you. Are you sure you're okay?" Jess added with a worried frown.

Sabina shrugged and smiled. "Just a little battle-scarred."

"What did you say to him?"

"I hit him," she said, noticing the wary look on Jess's face. "Then I dared the oil baron to hit me back."

Jess looked uneasy. "That wasn't wise. He has the memory of an elephant."

"He tried to buy me for the night," Sabina said curtly.

Jess made a soft sound. "Oh, my. No wonder you hit him! Good for you! Will you tell Al?"

She debated about that. "I'd rather not. Al doesn't know about my background. Just tell Al I'm not sorry I did it, but I'm sorry I embarrassed him."

"Al doesn't embarrass easily." Jessica toyed with the steering wheel. "I was pretty shocked when he asked me to hostess for him." She glanced up. "He's never invited me to his apartment before."

"He's started to notice you," Sabina said cautiously.

"Well, at least Thorn didn't toss me out tonight," Jess replied sadly. "He strikes me as a little snobbish where his family is concerned."

Sabina's temper flared again. "What he needs is someone who can put him in his place. And if he isn't careful, I may blacken his other eye for him!"

Jess laughed. "I can see it now—a TKO in the fifth round…"

"Good night," Sabina said, closing the car door behind her. She waved at Jess and went upstairs. Of all the unexpected endings to what had begun as a lovely evening. Closing the door of her apartment, she decided to skip dinner. She'd lost her appetite anyway. Sleep would be a welcome relief. But instead of losing herself to dreams, her mind replayed an image of Thorn and the way he'd kissed her. He'd touched her deeply, in ways she'd never expected to be touched.

How could she blame him for thinking she was easy, after the way she'd reacted to his unexpected ardor? He couldn't have known about her childhood, about her mother. She turned her hot face into the pillow. Now she'd made an enemy of him, and what was Al going to think? If only she'd stayed out of the kitchen, none of it would have happened.

She had a feeling she was going to be under siege shortly. The oil baron wasn't going to stand for having her in Al's life after this. She'd have bet money that he was already brooding about ways to get her away from Al, because she knew he had the impression that she and Al were more than friends. And part of her was even looking forward to the confrontation. She liked a sporting enemy.

before she knew he had the impression that
he would were quite out of focus. And part
of her was even now, in spite of the
memory, She almost cried out in a

Chapter Two

Sabina got up the next morning with a feeling
of dread. Immediately, her mind raced back to
the night before, and her heart burned at the
memory of a hard mouth invading hers.

It had been the first time she'd ever felt like
that. How ironic that it should be with a man
who was quickly becoming her worst enemy.
She had no inclination whatsoever for the light-
hearted alliances other women formed. She
knew too much about their consequences.

How odd, that Hamilton Thorndon the Third
should think that she was easy. She almost
laughed. If there was one woman in the world
his money couldn't get, it was Sabina.

With drooping eyelids she dragged herself into the exclusive Bourbon Street nightclub where she and the band were working. She'd never felt less like working, but the rehearsals went on regardless.

It was late afternoon, barely an hour from curtain time, and she was just finishing a tune about lost love, when Al came walking in. He looked as miserable as she felt, and his face looked sullen.

"Can you spare a minute?" Al asked.

"Sure," she said, jumping down from the stage in her satin shorts and top, and black leather boots. "Be right back!" she called to the boys.

Ricky Turner, the tall, thin bandleader and pianist, waved back. "Ten minutes, no more. We've still got two numbers to go over."

"Okay," she agreed. "He worries," she told Al as they sat down at a nearby table while around them busboys put out napkins and silver and glassware. "He's terrified that the stage will fall through, or the lights will come down on our heads, or that I'll trip over a cord and bash in the drums." She laughed softly. "Concerts are hard on Ricky's nerves. He's just started to relax since we've been doing this gig.''

"What happened last night?'' Al asked bluntly.

She flushed and averted her eyes. "Ask your brother.''

"I did. And he said the same thing. Look, if he hurt you…''

"I think I hurt him more,'' she said angrily. "I hit him just as hard as I could.''

His eyes widened. "Thorn? You hit Thorn?''

"Just as hard as…''

"I get the message. No wonder he was so icy.'' He studied her. "He wants to see you.''

Her mouth dropped. "Oh he does, does he? Did he say when?''

"In fifteen minutes. Now, before you go up in flames and say no, listen to me. I called my mother and told her I wanted to bring you to the ranch for a few days over Easter. She called Thorn and talked to him. Apparently he's ready to back down a little. I think all he wants is to issue you a personal invitation. But if you don't go to see him, everything's off. Including,'' he added gruffly, "my children's hospital benefit.

I can't get another backer. Without Thorn, we'll just have to do a one-night live concert at some theater. We won't raise nearly enough money that soon. I haven't told him much about the benefit. He won't even listen to me right now.''

"And you think he'll listen to *me*?" she said crisply. "And I don't think I want to spend Easter with your family."

"Sure you do. It'll be great fun. You'll like my mother."

"I'm sure I will, but I don't like your brother!"

He sighed. "The new hospital wing would cater to families who can't afford proper medical care," he said, eyeing her. "Especially children with fatal illnesses, like cancer. It would boast a research center as well."

Her eyes glittered at him. "Al..."

"Of course, it will eventually get built. In a few years. Meanwhile a lot of children will have to go to other cities, some won't be able to get treatment...."

"I'll do it, you animal," she said irritably. "You know I can't turn my back on any kind of benefit. But if your horrible brother tries to cut me up again, I'll paste him one!''

''That's the girl.'' He grinned. ''Get over to his office and give it to him!''

She left him to explain her departure to the band. She was just going out the door, still in costume, when she heard Ricky wail. Sabina quickened her pace and tried not to grin.

Minutes later, she paused at the door of the plush New Orleans office that housed Thorn Oil's executive officer. Taking a deep breath, she forced her racing heart to slow down. She told herself not to let her apprehension show or give the enemy any weakness to attack. Anyway, there was no reason to believe that old poisonous Hamilton Regan Thorndon the Third might want anything worse than a pleasant chat.

She laughed to herself. Sure. He just loved having the youngest son of the family mixed up with a rising young rock star and wanted to tell her so.

With a resigned sigh, she opened the door and walked into a lavish but sleek office, where a lovely blond receptionist was typing at a computer keyboard.

"Yes, may I help you?" she asked politely, smiling at Sabina.

"I'm here to see Hamilton Thorndon the Third," Sabina said, returning the smile. "I believe he's expecting me?"

The blonde looked wary as her eyes examined the slender figure in thigh-high black leather cuffed boots, tight pink satin shorts with a low-cut white satin camisole and silver-beaded vest under a thin jacket. Sabina almost chuckled. The outfit was so outrageous. But she had a performance in less than an hour and no time to change clothes, so the big man would just have to see her in her working garb. Her expression darkened with worry. She had grave misgivings about this. Especially after last night. But this business was best taken care of now. Thorn was the kind of man, from all description, who wouldn't mind walking up on the stage right in the middle of her nightclub performance to question her.

"Uh, I'll announce you," the blonde stammered, then buzzed the intercom. "Mr. Thorndon, there's a..." She put her hand over the receiver. "Your name, please?"

"Tell him it's Sabina," she replied in the clear voice that was her trademark.

"...Miss Sabina here. She says you're expecting her. Yes, sir." The receptionist hung up. "Mr. Thorndon will see you. Go right in."

Sabina was waved toward a door beside the desk. Smiling coyly at the blonde, she opened the door and poked her head in.

Immediately she regretted the lack of time to change into something more suitable. She'd have to bluff her way through. As usual.

"Here I am, your worship," she told the man behind the desk as she closed the door breezily behind her. "Fire away, but make it fast. I've got a performance in less than forty-five minutes."

He rose from the desk like a shark slicing through water, all sleek, smooth pursuit. The tan suit he was wearing did nothing to disguise the huge muscles of his arms, chest and legs. As he moved around the desk toward her, she felt his eyes sweep over her, as if she were being brushed all over with a flammable liquid.

His disposition was as cold as she remembered it. Sabina tried to block the previous night out of her mind while his blue, unblinking eyes were riveted on her.

A finger hit the intercom button. "No calls, honey."

"Yes, sir," came the edgy reply. Then there was silence while the oil magnate did what he was best at—intimidation.

He folded his arms across his chest and his blackened eye narrowed as he studied her graceful figure. "You do advertise it, don't you?" he murmured with a faint smile.

"This is my stage costume. Al said you wanted to see me immediately, and I just dropped everything and rushed right over. Satin is my trademark," she reminded him.

"So I've heard. How much do you want? What'll it cost for you to promise to leave Al alone?"

"Characteristically blunt," she remarked, eyeing him. "Have you ever found anything your money couldn't buy? Besides that oil refinery, I mean. Obviously, it's much more important than a little thing like Al's happiness."

An eyebrow jerked and the blackened eye squinted. She remembered that telltale signal, but she ignored it. "I hear through the grapevine that Al flew to Savannah to tell you about that singing engagement in my nightclub."

"Your nightclub?" she asked. "I understood that it was jointly owned by the two of you, and your mother."

At the mention of his mother, his body went rigid. "Al caused one hell of an argument last night. I do not want you at my ranch over the holidays. That's the one place I don't have to suffer women."

Her chin lifted. "I like Al," she told him. "And if he wants me to join him for Easter, I'll be delighted to accept." As she said that, she wondered vaguely why Al had invited her when Jessica had his whole heart. Was he trying to put up a smoke screen?

"Listen to me, you half-baked adventuress," he said suddenly. "I'm not having my brother taken over by a wild-eyed rock singer with eyes for his bankbook!" Moving toward her, he reached into his vest pocket, caught her roughly by the arm, and stuffed a piece of paper into the valley between her high breasts. "You take that and get the hell out of my brother's sight. I make a bad enemy. Remember it!"

He escorted her to the door and shoved her out of his office. "I'll make your apologies to my mother," he added sarcastically. The door slammed shut behind her.

The blonde stared at Sabina who stood there trembling, her face red and hot with hurt and humiliation, her eyes brimming with tears of fury. Just like old times, she thought wildly, just like my mother. She reached blindly for the check—she knew it was a check. Her trembling fingers unfolded it. It was made out to her, $20,000 worth. She stared at it for a long minute, until her face went purple.

Without a single regard for good sense, she whirled, opened the door to Thorn's office and stormed back in. She slammed the door behind her, watching his pale blue eyes widen with shock as his head jerked up.

She had a feeling that no one had ever dared cross him before. If she hadn't been so furious, she might have backed down, but it was too late for that now. Crossing the room with exquisite poise, she crumpled the check without looking at it, and threw it at him.

"You listen to me, you blue-eyed barracuda," she said, her eyes flashing venomously over the desk at him. "Al's invited me to the ranch, and I'm coming. You can take your bribe and stuff it up your arrogant nose!"

With a fierce look, he stood up and moved around the desk like a freight train barreling down a mountain.

She actually backed away, positioning herself behind the big leather sofa, her eyes widening with mingled fury and fear as he kept coming.

"Don't you do it, Hamilton Regan Thorndon the Third," she challenged, glaring at him. "You lay one hand on me, and I'll have you in court so fast your head will swim!"

"It will be worth it," he said, walking up onto the sofa, boots and all.

"You take your hands...!" she cried as he bounded over the leather back and jerked her into his arms. She never finished the sentence. He had her mouth under his, and he was hurting her.

She fought him, twisting, hitting him with her clenched hands. He backed her into the wall and held her there with the controlled weight of his body. After a moment or two, the bruising mouth relented a little and stopped demanding. It grew unexpectedly gentle, and as his hips pressed deeply against hers, she felt the sudden impact of his masculinity and caught her breath. He lifted his devouring mouth a breath away, and his hands slid down her waist to her hips, holding her as his eyes met hers. His chest rose and fell roughly, brushing her sensitive breasts.

"You're hurting me," she said unsteadily.

"And frightening you?" he asked quietly as he saw the apprehension in her eyes.

"Yes," she confessed.

He let her move away a little, so that the shocking evidence of his arousal was less noticeable. Her heart stopped pounding so feverishly. "Do you make...a habit of chasing women...over sofas in your office?" she asked breathlessly, trying to keep her sense of humor.

He didn't smile, but the corner of his mouth twitched. "No. Most of them have the good sense not to challenge me." He let her go with a rueful laugh. "On the other hand, I've never had a woman arouse me the way you do."

She averted her face to the window, trying to fight down the blush that was forming there.

"So I can't buy you off, is that what you're

telling me?'' he asked, moving away to his desk to light a cigarette.

"Chapter and verse," she proclaimed.

"There are other ways," he said, smoking quietly as he watched her smooth the hair his hands had angrily disheveled.

"Like seducing me?" she challenged, facing him. "No way. I'll never let you that close a second time."

"A third time," he corrected, and a faint gleam touched his eyes. "If you come out to the ranch, you could find yourself in a difficult position. Ask Al how I react to a challenge."

She didn't need to. She already knew. "You just want to choose Al's wife, is that it? You want him to marry a woman who would work to your advantage, of course, not his."

That eye narrowed again. "Think what you like about my motives. But you'll have to go through me to get to Al. Give it up before anyone gets hurt."

"Threats?" she chided.

"Promises." He took a draw from the cigarette and something alien flared in his blue eyes. "I'm a reasonable man. You can still have the check if you want it. No strings. How's that for generosity?''

She stared at him, calculating. ''Suppose I show up at the ranch for Easter?''

He took another draw from the cigarette. ''Try it.''

She pursed her lips. That check would go a long way toward Al's goal for the children's hospital wing. And it would needle the hell out of this overprotective oil magnate. She held out her hand.

He looked faintly disappointed, even as he reached for the check, yet he tossed it to her with careless accuracy. ''Smart girl.''

''You don't realize how smart. Yet,'' she added. She blew him a kiss and walked out. ''Have a nice day,'' she called to the blonde secretary as she breezed out of the office.

An hour later, Sabina went onto the stage at the exclusive Bourbon Street nightclub feeling wildly reckless. Consequently, she gave the best performance of her short career. The band beat out the thick rhythm, and Sabina, in her satin and sequins, sang in her piercingly clear voice, every word discernible, her body throbbing with the drums. She could feel the music, actually feel it, and the overflowing audience seemed to feel it with her, clapping and keeping time with her, smiling appreciatively as she took them with her to the heady finale. She moved across the stage, bathed in colored lights, and held her audience spellbound as the last notes died. In the audience, Al watched her with a worried frown.

After the final set, she walked off the stage and sat down with him. Anger still glittering in her eyes.

"What's wrong?" he asked quietly.

"Read me pretty well, don't you, my friend?" she asked. She ordered a cup of coffee from the waiter and smiled at Al. "Your brother and I went two more rounds."

"Again? For God's sake! I should have known better," he growled, running a hand through his hair. "I never learn, never!"

She pulled the check out of her pocketbook and showed it to him. "This is how much he thinks you're worth to me. I'd be insulted if I were you. You're worth a hundred thousand, at least!"

Al's face went bloodred and he started shaking. "I'll break his head," he hissed.

"I'll get you a hammer."

"You didn't turn around and throw it at him?" he asked, watching her fiddle with it.

She burst out laughing. "Of course I did." She grinned, neglecting to mention what had happened next. "Then he dared me to come to the ranch, and I told him hell itself wouldn't keep me away. How's that for friendship?"

He let out a breath. "My gosh! You got away with it?" He laughed. "Sabina, you're the greatest!" he said enthusiastically. "Are you coming with me, really?"

"Sure."

He seemed to grow an inch. "Fantastic." He eyed her. "Now, if I can just sell you on the rest of the plan. By the way, what are you going to do with that check?"

She unfolded the $20,000 check. "I'm giving this to you for your new project. In your awful brother's name, of course." She smiled at Al's expression as she endorsed it and handed it to him.

He took it, but his eyebrows arched. "But he'll think you took the bribe!"

"Let him," she said, leaning back.

He started to laugh. "He'll be out for blood. You haven't ever seen Thorn in action."

Want to bet? she thought amusedly. "I've lived dangerously all my life."

He reached across and caught her hand in his thin one. "Prodding Thorn isn't any way to get even. He could hurt you."

"Because he's rich?" she asked with a laugh.

"No. Because he's Thorn. Money doesn't make any difference whatsoever."

"I hate being made a fool of," she muttered. "I hate being humiliated. He's not getting away with that. I'd dearly love to pay him off."

His eyes wandered over her face. "Do you really want to get even with him and help me out at the same time?"

"Of course!" she said without hesitation.

"Then let me buy you an engagement ring."

Sabina all but fainted. The look on her face spoke volumes, and Al couldn't help laughing.

"No, you've got it all wrong. I'm very fond of you. I'm sure you're fond of me. But I don't have marriage in mind."

"A bogus engagement, then?"

"Exactly." He chuckled softly. "I'm so damned tired of having Thorn scare away girlfriends because he doesn't think I can manage my own love life. I'd purely enjoy setting him down hard for once. He's only ten years my senior, but he acts as if he were my father."

"How old did you say he was?" she asked curiously.

"Thirty-four."

"Are you really only twenty-four?" she asked, grinning. "I thought you were at least sixty."

"Shame on you. Attacking a man who's trying to assist you in a monumental vendetta!"

"What would I have to do?" she asked, pursing her lips.

"Be seen everywhere with me. Especially," he added with a hot grin, "at the ranch. That would kill him."

"What about your mother? I'd hate to play such a trick on her."

"Oh, she'd be no problem. She spends most of her time in Europe, especially since our father died ten years ago. Odd thing, Thorn was effortlessly running Thorn Oil at my age. And here am I fighting tooth and nail to keep from being taken over.''

"You're not like him," she said quietly. "And I mean it as a compliment."

He cocked his head and smiled slightly. "Do you? Most women find him fascinating and wildly sexy."

"I don't like domineering men," she said flatly. "I can run my own life without being told what to do. I rebelled at an early age."

"I wish I had. I was too busy learning the oil business at Thorn's knee to fight being overrun." He smiled sheepishly. "Now that I want to cut the strings, I'm finding that they're pretty tough. I don't come into the trust until I'm twenty-five. That gives brother Thorn another year of absolute domination."

"And then?"

"Then I'll have a sizable share of stock and enough money to start my own damned oil company, if I feel like it." He brought her hand to his lips and kissed it gently. "Help me declare independence. Wear my ring for a few weeks and watch Thorn paw the ground."

"As long as he doesn't try to paw me," she

said with a hearty laugh. "I'd rather take poison."

He studied her flushed face quietly. "He really got under your skin, didn't he?"

She shrugged. "It was bad enough at that party. But today was the biggest slap in the face I've had since I was a kid." She looked up. "I'll wear the ring for you. But make it something inexpensive, okay? And something you can return!"

"Will do!" He chuckled.

The ring he brought her the following day was an emerald, not too flashy but surrounded with diamonds in a platinum setting. She gasped.

"Remember that I'm not a poor man," he said before she could protest. "To me, this is an inexpensive ring."

She slid it onto her finger, shaking her head. "When I think of all the heating bills it would pay for my neighbors..."

"No," he said. "Absolutely not. You can't hock the ring."

She laughed delightedly, her eyes sparkling. "I wouldn't, you know. But I feel kind of guilty wearing it all the same."

"It suits you. Emeralds make your skin look creamy." He hesitated a moment. "Thorn called me."

She felt her face draw into a scowl as her mood darkened. "Did he?"

He leaned back in his chair with a drink in hand. "I told him I'd just bought you a ring."

"What did he say?"

"I don't know. I hung up in the middle of it." He chuckled. "He was fit to be tied!"

"When do we leave for the ranch?" she asked apprehensively.

"Day after tomorrow."

"So soon?" she murmured, her eyes and voice plaintive.

"I'll protect you, don't worry," he promised. "We'll only be there a few days. Besides, Thorn doesn't spend a lot of time at the ranch, even on holidays. Especially now."

"Because of me?" She felt unwanted and nervous as she studied the ring. "Maybe this isn't such a good idea, Al."

"You can't back out now," he said merrily. "I'll sue you for breach of contract."

Sabina burst out laughing. "Oh, you," she muttered. Her breasts rose and fell with a heavy sigh. "Al, I'm afraid of him," she admitted softly.

"Yes, I know." His eyes were calculating. It was the first time he'd ever seen her afraid of any man, and he wondered why. "Sabina, he won't hurt you. Not physically."

Her lower lip trembled. Hating that tiny betrayal and fearing that Al would notice, she got up from the table. "I'll be packed and ready to go," she promised. "Now I'd better get some sleep. Walk me home?"

"I'll drive you," he said. "Don't worry. It will be all right."

She hoped he was on target with that prediction. She truly was afraid of Hamilton Regan Thorndon the Third, and he hated her. This was an insane thing to do; she needed her head examined. Of course, maybe he wouldn't be at the ranch. She comforted herself with that hope. Then she realized something else.

"Jessica!" she burst out as he pulled up in front of her apartment house.

He stared curiously. "What?"

She swallowed. "Uh, I was just wondering what people will think."

"That's not what you said. Sabina, please. What's going on?"

The painfully hopeful expression on his face made her come out with it. Jess would kill her, but maybe it would be worth it. "She'll kill me for telling you. But..." she sighed, eyeing him. "Well, you see, Jess is in love with you."

He seemed struck dumb. At a loss for words, he stared at the dashboard as if he'd never seen it. His fingers toyed with the key in the ignition. "She is?"

Sabina didn't reply. She just sat and watched him. He took a deep breath and began to smile.

"Are you sure?" he asked, glancing at her.

She nodded, smiling back.

"Damn!" He took another deep breath. "Jess...." Then the sudden exaltation faded and his face fell. "What difference does it make now? Thorn won't let me have her. She doesn't have an oil refinery."

"I'm going to be the decoy, remember?" She grinned at him, flashing the emerald. "Go tell Jess you just got engaged to me. She's home alone tonight. I was going to have a late cup of coffee with her after the show. You can go instead of me."

He frowned and then smiled. "Well—"

"Go on, for Pete's sake! Thorn won't know unless you tell him!"

He shrugged. "Well—"

"Faint heart never won, etc., etc.," she quoted.

"You're right." He glanced at her. "You aren't afraid to go through with this?"

Sabina shook her head. Inside she was trembling, but no one would ever know it. Jess was her best friend. Al was as much to her. She could do this one thing for them. Besides, she thought angrily, it would do the oil baron good to be set on his heels for once. And she was just the girl to do it.

"Okay. Here goes nothing. See you tomorrow."

She got out of the car. "Don't blow it, Romeo," she teased.

He made a face at her and pulled back out into traffic, preoccupied and thoughtful. She thought about calling Jess to warn her. But then she reasoned that Jess was a divorcé with a sharp mind, and didn't. Jessica could take care of herself. Or, at least, that's what she thought until the next morning.

Just as she was having her first cup of coffee, there was a hard knock on the door.

She got up and opened it, shocked to find Jessica standing there, her eyes red-rimmed, her red hair disheveled.

"Jess!" she burst out. "What's wrong?"

"Everything," came the wailing reply. "Can I have some coffee, please?"

"Of course." Sabina pulled her robe closer and got a second cup from the cupboard. When she came back into the room, Jessica was sitting at the small table with her head in her hands. "What happened?"

"Doesn't it show?"

Sabina took a long, hard look at her best friend, shocked by her unruly appearance, the dark shadows under her eyes.

"Al and you…?" Sabina said.

"Bingo!" Jessica poured herself a cup of coffee and sipped it nervously. She looked up with a pained expression. "What did you say to Al last night?"

Sabina blinked. "Nothing." She lied.

"You must have said something, you must have," Jessica moaned. She put the coffee cup down. "He came to the apartment. He was passing, he said, and thought I might have a spare cup of coffee. You know how I feel, how I've felt for months. Well, he said you and he had just got engaged, and I went crazy. I threw a lamp at him and swore.'' She smiled sheepishly. ''Well, one thing led to another, and he kissed me. Then he told me the engagement was just to throw Thorn off the track. And he kissed me again.'' She drew in a short breath. ''Oh, my, oh, my, I guess it blew my mind, because when he started toward the bedroom, I followed. It was the shortest night of my whole life. Now I can't go home because he's still there, and I'm afraid to go to the office. I'm afraid he'll think I'm cheap, and I'm so much more in love with him this morning than I ever imagined I could be!''

Sabina's face lit up as she laughed and hugged her friend. ''He cares!'' she said. ''He does; he has to. You know Al, for God's sake! He'd never take you to bed on an impulse; he's too deep.''

''But he'll think I'm easy!'' Jessica wailed.

''Wanna bet?'' Sabina went to the phone, throwing herself down into the armchair beside it. She dialed Jess's number.

"No, you can't!" Jessica screamed, diving for the phone.

Sabina struggled with her, grinning. "No, you don't. Be quiet!"

It rang and rang until Al answered it drowsily. "Hello?"

"Hi, Al," Sabina said.

"Hi." He moaned, then all of a sudden, there was an exclamation. "Jess!" he burst out. "Sabina, is Jess with you? Oh, God, what she must have thought.... Is she there?"

"Yes," Sabina said, watching Jess hide her face in her hands. "She is. And feeling pretty low."

"Oh, God, the fat's in the fire now," Al groaned. "Thorn will send her to Siberia the second he knows... Let me talk to her, please!"

"He wants to talk to you," Sabina said, handing the phone to her nervous friend. "Go on. He sounds frantic."

Jessica took it. "Hello," she said unsteadily, brushing back her hair. "Yes. Oh, yes." She began to calm down. She smiled. "Yes." Jess sat down in the chair and Sabina left the room.

Sabina sipped her coffee in the tiny kitchen.

Minutes later, Jessica came through the door, looking subdued and happy and sad, all at once.

"I'm going home to talk to him," she said. "But it seems pretty hopeless. Thorn wants him to marry the oil refinery, you see." She shrugged. "I guess a divorced nobody of a secretary wouldn't be good enough." She looked up. "Listen, you weren't sweet on Al, were you?"

"Al and I are just buddies. In the beginning we worked up this false engagement to get big brother off his back. But now it may serve a different purpose. As for being sweet on anyone... You know what it was like for me when I was growing up. You know I don't want involvement, and you know why."

"Yes," Jess sighed sadly. "I understand. It's just that I wish you could be as happy as I am, my friend." She picked up her purse. "I'd better go. Al said he wasn't going to work until we talked. I think he and Thorn got into a spat yesterday over the refinery heiress again."

"Big brother just radiates love, doesn't he?" Sabina said coldly.

"He's trouble. Watch out."

"You're the one who'd better take that advice," Sabina murmured. "I'm just the red herring. You're the fox." She grinned.

"Some fox." Jessica laughed. "Don't take any chances. You're the best friend I ever had."

"Same here." Sabina flashed the engagement ring. "I'll keep this warm for you," she added wickedly.

Jess only laughed. "It wasn't funny when he first told me. But now, I think it's just great!"

"I wish I could have seen your face."

"It was a fascinating shade of purple," Jessica grinned as she headed for the door. "Thanks for the coffee!"

"Any time," Sabina murmured dryly. "See you later."

Jessica barely nodded, and then she was gone.

But if Sabina thought that was going to be the end of it, she had a surprise waiting the next evening after her performance. Al and Jess were waiting for her, all eyes and expectations after she'd changed into her street clothes and grabbed her long secondhand cashmere coat and joined them at their table.

"Hi." Jess grinned.

"Yes, hi," Al seconded.

She studied them with pursed lips. "You look like crocodiles with your eyes on a fat chicken. What have you cooked up that's going to get me in trouble?"

"You volunteered," Al reminded her with a laugh.

She glared at the engagement ring on her finger. "Yes, but I'm only keeping it warm for Jess."

"Jess and I are going to get married next week," Al said.

Sabina perked up at that. She beamed, then almost cried at the look of happiness on their faces. "Marvelous!"

"Once we've actually done it, there's not a thing big brother can do to me," Al said. "Besides that, there's this tricky little loophole in the trust—if I get married, I inherit the trust immediately." He looked gloriously happy. "Thorn will never be able to tell me what to do again. And Jess and I can stop worrying about Thorn's matchmaking attempts."

"So I'm to divert him, is that it?" she asked.

Al nodded. "We'll be in Beaumont at the ranch for several days, but with Mother and me to run interference for you, it will be okay. He's in and out of the ranch because of his responsibilities and while he's working I'll sneak out with Jess to make the arrangements."

Sabina was thoughful. Of course she wanted to help, but crossing Thorn this way could backfire. She hadn't forgotten the way she'd felt in his arms, and she didn't like being vulnerable. He probably knew how he affected her. She wouldn't put anything past him, especially if he thought the engagement was for real. He'd stoop pretty low to save his brother, and she was uneasy about the tactics he might use.

"We leave tomorrow morning, you know," Al reminded her.

"Yes, but what about the performances...?"

"We've got a vocalist to fill in for you," Al responded quickly. "I'm sorry, I know you don't like that, but Thorn did mention that if you were going to be at the ranch, it wasn't practical for you to commute back and forth for the week.''

She felt a burning sensation. ''Will I have a job to go back to?'' she asked.

''Of course,'' Al said. But he didn't look that confident. He swore softly. ''Damn, Sabina, I'm sorry. I'm not up to Thorn's weight. My God, who is?''

''I'll discuss it with him while we're at the ranch,'' Sabina said. She even managed to laugh. She couldn't blame Al for being himself. Her protective instincts were what had drawn her to him in the first place. He was like a baby brother. And she loved Jessica too much to pull out now. She could handle the oil baron. She'd just be a decoy, after all. ''I'd better go pack!'' she said with a smile. ''Now, Jess, don't worry about a thing. I'll make sure big brother doesn't take a single bite out of your intended.''

Jess got up and hugged her warmly. ''I love you,'' she said fervently. ''Please be careful.'' She looked at Sabina, and her eyes said it all. ''You're much more vulnerable than anyone realizes.''

Sabina straightened. ''Don't worry, I believe

in self-preservation. See you in the morning, Al!'' she called.

"You're a pal," he told her, and he meant it.

"I'm a nut case," she muttered to herself as she left. She had a feeling this was going to be the worst mistake of her life—like prodding a cobra with a straw.

Chapter Three

The Thorndon ranch was just outside Beaumont, Texas, surrounded by white fences and hugh oak and pecan trees. The house was a two-story Victorian model, gleaming white, with intricate gingerbread woodwork and a huge front porch and a lawn that was glorious in spring. The trees were bare now, because it was late autumn, but Sabina could picture it in warm weather with flowers all around. She'd seen a house like that in a storybook at the orphanage when she was a little girl, and she used to dream of living in one. Her eyes were wide and sad as she studied the sleek lines of the Rolls-Royce parked in the driveway. The oil baron's car, no doubt, she thought bitterly. He had so much, and she'd had so little all her life. Her father must have been just such a man....

"This is home," Al told her, stopping his Mercedes-Benz just as a solitary rider came into view against the backdrop of the trees. Wearing a tan sheepskin coat and a creamy wide-brimmed hat, the rider sat astride the most magnificent black stallion Sabina had ever seen.

The rider was coming toward them at a gallop, through a herd of white-faced, red-coated Herefords, so close to his horse that they seemed to be irrevocably joined. Sabina watched him, fascinated, and wondered if he was one of the cowhands who worked for the Thorndons. That lean, easy grace spoke of hours in the saddle.

"He rides beautifully, doesn't he?" Al murmured. "I remember watching him when we were boys and wishing I could do it half as well. He used to ride in rodeo competition, but then Dad died and he had to take over the oil company. I don't think he's really been happy since."

Sabina frowned slightly as the meaning of the words penetrated. The solitary rider had closed the gate he'd just ridden through and remounted, coming near enough that his face was recognizable. He cocked his hat over one eye and gave Sabina a slow, insolent smile. The black eye had lost some of its vividness. Now just a faint discoloration attested to its existence.

"Hello, rock singer," Hamilton Regan Thorndon the Third said mildly. "Fancy you on a ranch, cream puff."

She looked at him expressionlessly, as if he were a faintly interesting exhibit in a museum. "Yes, I know, I'll just be bored silly. But I'll muddle through somehow, oil baron," she said with a sweet smile.

He didn't like that cool appraisal or the taunting words, and his eyes narrowed as he lit a cigarette.

"How's it going?" Al asked casually.

"Feed's low," Thorn said. "We'll have to supplement the stock through the winter. I've sold off the culls already."

"That's the cattle business for you," the younger man agreed. "Is Mother here yet?"

Thorn's face grew colder. "She isn't coming."

Al stared at him. "Not coming?"

"The new boyfriend doesn't want to come all this way for a holiday," the older man said with a mirthless laugh. He drew on the cigarette. "And Mother doesn't want to leave him. Early days, you know."

"I'm sorry," Al said. "I'd hoped... It's been over a year since she's set foot on the ranch."

"She doesn't like the smell of cattle." Thorn's eyes went to Sabina, chilling blue eyes. "You won't be able to wear satin shorts around here, honey," he added.

"Okay." She shrugged. "I'll just go naked. Al won't mind," she said with a grin.

Thorn threw his cigarette to the ground. "You'll have separate rooms here," he told them. "And no midnight wandering, or so help me God, I'll throw both of you out the door!"

He turned his horse without another word, leaving Sabina spellbound.

"Whew!" Al sighed, easing the car up the driveway. "Mother really must have upset him this time."

"Does Thorn resemble her?" Sabina asked curiously.

"He looks like our father," he said. "A mirror image. Sometimes he acts like him, too. Dad was a passionate man, but he had a core of pure steel, and he used it on everybody. He could send our mother into tears with a look and keep her that way for days if he was angry. She got even, in the most basic way."

She stared at him. "Other men?"

His face darkened. "Other men. Thorn's always hated her for it, and she knows it. I think that's why she stays away. She can't really help the way she is, I suppose, but Thorn never forgave her for betraying Dad." He glanced at her after he'd parked the car behind the Rolls. "Dad caught her with one of her lovers. He dragged her out of the hotel, threw her into his car, and was driving her home in a rage when he wrecked the car. He was killed."

Sabina bit her lower lip. "How old was Thorn?"

"Twenty-four. My age. I'll never forget the way he looked at Mother, or what he said to her. She left the ranch just after the funeral and went to live with an aunt in England."

She shivered. So he knew, too. He knew. Her eyes closed.

"What is it?" Al asked, concerned.

"Nothing," she murmured. "Just a chill." She pulled her coat closer around her. Under it, she was wearing her only pair of cowboy boots, with designer jeans and a bulky gray sweater over a white blouse. The jeans and sweater, like the coat, were from the nearly new shop, and Al just shook his head as he studied her.

"You amaze me," he said. "You always look like something out of Rodeo Drive, but you hardly pay anything for it."

"I know where to look," she said with a grin. "Let's go. I'm just getting warmed up."

"Thorn bites when he's in this mood," he cautioned her. "Don't underestimate him. Stick close to me."

"You can count on it."

The house was misleading. Judging by its front, it was a bastion of quiet elegance. But inside it was a masculine stronghold. The living room was done in earthy tones, with Indian rugs and a strong Mexican influence as well. The walls in the living room and den were pecan-paneled, and hunting trophies and rodeo awards lined the wall of the den.

"Thorn's," Al told her, quiet pride in his voice. "He always took top money. The men still gather around when he feels like a little bronc busting out in the corral. It's quite a sight."

"How big is the ranch?" she asked.

"Not very, by Texas standards. But it's a good place to relax, and Thorn likes to experiment with his purebred Herefords. He's very much into embryo transplants right now, genetic improvement."

That was Greek to Sabina. She'd spent a little time with her grandfather, her mother's father, who had a farm just outside New Orleans. But that was years ago, before the old man died. She had just a few pleasant memories of being allowed to ride horses and breathe clean, country air and gaze toward an uncluttered horizon.

Her fingers lightly touched one of the awards, feeling its cold metal surface. It chilled her, like the man who'd earned it. "He must be very proud of these," she told Al.

"He is," came a deep voice from the doorway.

She turned to find Thorn, long-legged, narrow-hipped, devastating in jeans and a half-unbuttoned blue plaid shirt. He was still wearing dusty boots and the wide-brimmed hat that emphasized his dark complexion. His blue eyes were piercing from across the room, and his chiseled lips turned up in a twisted mockery of a smile.

"The metal is an alloy; they aren't worth much," he told her, oblivious of Al's glare.

"How sad," she sighed, moving away. "You couldn't even hock them if you needed money, could you, Hamilton Regan Thorndon the Third?"

"My name is Thorn," he said in a tone laced with authority.

She looked up, tossing back her long, silky hair. "That's what your friends call you, I'm sure," she said. "I am not, and never will be, your friend. I will call you Hamilton or Mr. Thorndon the Third or Hey, You. Take your pick."

His eyes were flashing with anger, but she didn't even flinch. He pursed his lips. "Declaring war, honey? Watch out. You're on my turf now.''

"I don't have a white flag to my name," she returned with deliberate provocation. Honey. She hated that silky endearment that she'd heard so often in her youth. "And don't call me honey, your worship."

"My God, you're brave," he said tartly.

She corrected him. "I just don't like being walked on," she said, never letting her gaze waver.

His blue eyes searched her face for a long, static moment, while he seemed to be trying to read her mind.

She laughed. "Looking for weak links? I don't have any. I'm every bit as hard as you are."

"You'll need to be," he said.

Recognizing the tone, Al stiffened. "Uh, Sabina, let's see the rest of the house."

She turned her eyes away from Thorn, feeling a weakness in her knees. She had had this tingling feeling for a few seconds, but she didn't dare let him know it.

"Sure," she told Al, taking his hand quickly.

"I'm opening up a new oil field out on the western stretch of the property," Thorn told his brother. "Ride out there with me."

"Now? Like this?" Al asked, indicating his gray suit.

"Change first."

"Want to come along, Sabina?" Al asked.

"She rides?" Thorn laughed mockingly.

"*She* sure does," Sabina said with a deliberate vacant smile. "*She* even speaks all by herself, without help."

"I'll just get my suitcase out of the car. Be right back." Al told Sabina with a smile and a wink. As he walked out, she had to fight the urge to run after him.

"You make everything a challenge, don't you?" she asked Thorn after a minute.

His gaze almost knocked the breath out of her. "Honey, you're a walking challenge," he said. "And if you aren't careful, baby brother or no baby brother, I'm going to take you up on it."

"I'm not issuing an invitation. I have wonderful instincts for self-preservation," she replied as lightly as she could.

He drew a cigarette out of his pocket and lit

it without taking his gaze off her. "What a hell of an irony," he said with a cold laugh. "That night in Al's kitchen, I'd never touched anything so sweet. And not five minutes later, I had to face what you actually were."

Her temperature was rising. "I'm a rock singer," she told him coldly. "Not a tramp. My profession has nothing to do with my morals."

His breath came deeply, as though he were deliberately controlling it. The cigarette fired trails of smoke between his lean fingers. "I won't let you marry Al," he said forcefully. "I'll do anything I have to do, but I'll stop you."

"Anything?" she challenged.

He nodded slowly. "Within limits," he said quietly, letting his eyes wander slowly down her body. "Don't make me hurt you, Sabina." His voice was deep and as smooth as velvet as he watched her. "You can't help what you are, I suppose. But I want Al married for something more than his bankroll."

Her face dropped. "You think I'm a gold digger?"

"I know you are," he said. "Remember the check for twenty thousand that I gave you?"

She wanted to tell him what she'd done with it. But that would lead to other questions, questions she didn't want to answer. He might get the truth out of her in a weak moment, and where would that leave Al and Jessica?

"If you'll do what I ask, I'll forget the check," he said. "And I'll get you all the performances you and the band can handle. All you have to do is leave Al alone."

"But, he's such a sweet little feller," she murmured with a wicked smile. "Besides, he turns me on, you know?"

He moved closer, so that she could feel the warmth of his body, and the wild longings it produced tricked her into looking up. His eyes trapped hers. His free hand moved to her face and lightly touched her mouth. The slight sensation made it tremble.

"Stop that. You're no more an experienced woman than I am a monk. I've had women. And if you're not damned careful, I'll have you."

"After I've been embalmed, maybe," she

retorted. "And will you please remember that I'm engaged to Al?" she said too quickly.

His fingers were under her chin, sensually tracing the long line of her throat, and she could taste his smoky breath on her lips, feel the strength, warmth and power of his lean body and smell his cologne and faint leathery scent.

"Sure you are. For now." He traced his fingers over her soft cheek, down to the curve of her lips. He drew in a slow, heavy breath. "Skin like milk," he whispered. "Soft mouth, even if it doesn't quite know how to kiss."

Her eyelids felt heavy, her body felt weak. She looked up at him and couldn't look away.

He dropped his hand abruptly, as if the contact with her skin was disturbing to him. "I'm not gentle," he said abruptly. "There's never been a woman who could make me gentle. I like it rough, and I don't hold anything back. And that's the last thing you need, cream puff. I won't seduce you. That's not my way. But I could lose my head with you, so keep a few yards away from me while you're here, okay? It would be hell living with myself if I seduced a virgin."

She couldn't even move, the words were such a shock.

"Yes, I know," he said softly, searching her eyes. "It doesn't go with your image, or even with the other things I know about you. But I'd stake my life on your innocence." His eyes fell to her mouth, lingered there. "It would have been so easy, I even had it planned. Now I'll have to find some other way."

"I don't understand."

"I'm ruthless. Didn't Al tell you? I always get my own way. Always." He sighed angrily. "Except with you. If you'd been the experienced little tart I thought you were, I could have seduced you and told Al, and that would have been the end of it."

Her eyes were lost in his. "You'd go that far?" she asked quietly.

He nodded. "He's my brother. I love him, in my way." His gaze silenced her. "He's the only thing I do love, so look out. You chose to ignore the warning I gave you. You took a bribe and welched on it."

"Did I?" she murmured, staring up at him. "Why don't you tell Al?"

"Not just yet," he replied, his eyes promising dark delights. "I'm going to bide my time. Maybe it will be worth the twenty thousand to have you off the place."

His eyes were the coldest she'd ever seen. If he was vulnerable in any way, it didn't show, but she could almost picture him as a child. She'd have bet that he was a loner from the beginning, a quiet, confident child who wouldn't be pushed by anyone. He'd probably done his share of fighting because of his mother.

"Why are you looking at me like that?" he asked, his tone jarring.

"I'm sorry we're enemies," she said with her irrespressible honesty. "I'd have liked you for a friend."

His face got even sterner. "I don't have friends. Men or women."

"Did it ever occur to you that not everybody in the world is after you for what they can get?"

He burst out with laughter that was cynical and mocking. "You're just the person to tell me about that, aren't you, honey? You, with your eyes like dollar signs!"

"Sabina?" Al called.

She turned and quickly fled from the den without looking at Thorn. "Here I am," she called. "I'll freshen up and meet you back down here, okay?" she told him, as she ran up the staircase. Al followed, frowning thoughtfully.

Remembering what Thorn had said to her made her knees go weak. The threats she understood; he was trying to protect his brother. Ironically, so was she. But in spite of it all, how had he known she was a virgin, when all his imagined evidence pointed in the opposite direction? She turned away from the mirror, forcing herself not to ask impossible questions. All she had to remember was that Thorn was the enemy. If she forgot, he could destroy any hope of Al's marriage to Jessica. She had to keep that in mind. If only it wasn't so difficult to hate him. He was a rich man, like those she'd known in her childhood, like the last one in her mother's tragic life.... She shuddered a little at the black memory, but even that couldn't get the oil baron out of her mind. Somehow, she felt a kinship with him. She understood him. She wore a mask, too, and shunned emotional involvement. What a pity they were in opposite camps.

Chapter Four

Sabina hadn't ridden a horse in a long time, but she sat on the little mare Thorn gave her with grace. It had been a long time, but she remembered very well how to ride. Her grandfather had taken care of her for a year or two, until he died, and he'd been a good rider himself. It had been the happiest period of her life. She'd loved her grandfather dearly, and mourned terribly when she lost him.

The country around the ranch was fascinating. Not too many miles away was the Big Thicket, a fascinating junglelike area where orchids grew wild. Early in the 1800s it had been a trapping outpost. Nearby were the ruins of a

French trading post. After that came lumber and rice plantations. And in the early 1900s, oil was discovered in the Spindletop Oilfield. Beaumont became the birthplace of three major oil companies. Four, if Thorn Oil was included. The Sabine River, which led into Orange, east of Beaumont, was the origin of Sabina's name. Her father, she understood, had lived on its banks as a boy.

As they were coming back from a look at some land where men were setting up a drilling rig, Thorn had explained it to Sabina with unexpected patience. She had been openly fascinated by it. Al had grinned, watching them, because he'd never seen Thorn so approachable. Al himself looked different in Western gear, except that his jeans were new and had a designer label, and his gray hat was smothered in feathers. Next to Thorn, in his worn and obviously used outfit, he seemed citified. "It's great out here," Al told his brother.

"I'm glad you said that," Thorn drawled, cocking his hat over one eye. "I'll let you help us brand the replacement heifers."

"It's not that great, Thorn," came the quick reply, with a grin.

"So I figured. You need to get out here more often. Sitting behind that desk all the time isn't healthy. Neither is all the partying," he added with a pointed glance at Sabina.

"Al doesn't party." She defended Al, not looking at Thorn. "He has parties."

"Is there a difference?" he drawled.

Al interrupted. "That's all over, anyway. When Sabina and I get married, I won't have the time anymore."

That set the big man off. He reined in his horse and stared at Al until the shorter man visibly fidgeted.

"Marriage is a big step. What about her career?" he asked pointedly. "Is she going to give it all up to stay home with you?"

"So what if she wants to work? What's wrong with a woman being independent?" Al asked.

"Not a damned thing," his brother agreed, "until her independence interferes with your own. Do you like the way other men leer at her in those body stockings she wears?"

"I wouldn't call it leering," Al muttered.

"Well, I would," Thorn said flatly. He crossed his tanned forearms over the pommel and glared at Sabina. "And what are you offering him? Your spare time? I understand you're on the road most of it."

That was a question she hadn't thought about. Her music was part of her life; giving it up was impossible. But she was supposed to be engaged...it was time to think fast. "Well, I guess I'll just stay home and have babies," she sighed, and looked up in time to catch an odd expression in the oil baron's eyes. He let his gaze drop down her body, till he was eyeing her midriff. He frowned before he caught her eyes again. Incredibly, she blushed.

"Are we going to see the rest of the ranch now?" she asked quickly. "I'm getting hungry."

"The old timers," Al murmured with a grin, "used to butcher a cow along the way."

"Beef on the hoof," Sabina said with an evil smile in Thorn's direction. "Walking steaks..."

"Touch one of my purebred Herefords and I'll take your arm off," Thorn replied with a faint smile.

"Spoilsport," she muttered. "Some host you are."

"They're purebred, dammit!" Thorn laughed reluctantly.

"Okay. Tell you what," she said agreeably. "I'll eat the registration papers with it."

His blue eyes twinkled unexpectedly. Al had to stifle a smile of his own. It had been years since he'd seen Thorn like that. The older man was grim most of the time; he hardly ever cracked a smile. Sabina was working subtle witchcraft on Thorn.

She sighed and shrugged. "Well, if I faint from lack of food, and fall onto a rattlesnake, and get bitten and die, just remember, it's all your fault."

Thorn held back another laugh and turned his stallion. "Come on, for God's sake, and I'll feed you."

He spurred his horse and rode ahead of them to open a gate. Sabina's eyes followed him helplessly, her heart spinning in her chest, a bright new feeling making her light-headed with elation.

"He never laughs," Al said under his breath. "That's a first."

"He's just forgotten how," Sabina said, and her eyes were soft on the tall man's back. "Jess said that deep inside he was a lonely man, and I didn't believe her. Now I do.''

"He's lonely from choice," he reminded her, concerned. "Don't go soft on him, Sabina. You never know with Thorn. He'll get your guard down, and then he'll strike. I've seen it happen far too often.''

"I'll be careful," she promised. After all, it was just a game, wasn't it? "Don't forget to invite me to the wedding.''

Al grinned. "You can give her away, if you like," he teased.

She glared at him. "How did I ever get friends like you?''

"Pure luck," he returned smugly. Sabina laughed and rode after Thorn.

They didn't dress up for dinner that night, although Sabina had halfway expected that they would. Nevertheless, she wore a gray skirt and blue-and-white checked blouse instead of jeans.

Thorn was alone in the living room, brooding over his drink. The white pullover sweater he was wearing with his dark slacks emphasized his own deep tan and black hair. As if he felt her watching him, his head turned and his icy blue eyes met hers.

"Where's your satin, rock star?" he chided.

"I didn't want to risk having your heart stop, Mr. Thorndon the Third," she said with a wicked smile as she joined him.

He caught her arm with a lean, steely hand and held her as she tried to walk past him. "I've told you that I don't like that name," he said in a tone softly laced with menace. "Don't push me. It's dangerous."

She could feel the danger, and she regretted her barb almost as she'd said it. "Mr. Thorndon, then," she said softly. "Will you let me go, please?"

"Did it hurt to ask?" he chided, abruptly releasing her arm. He turned away. "What will you drink?"

"I don't."

He whirled. "You what?"

"I told you at Al's party. I hate alcohol."

He scowled down at her. "A social drink isn't considered alcoholism."

"I'm sure it isn't, and I'm not sitting in judgment," she assured him. "I simply do not like the taste of liquor."

He shrugged. "Suit yourself, tulip."

"What?" she broke out.

"Tulip," he repeated. His pale gaze wandered over her face, down to the deep, full red of her mouth. "Maybe someday I'll tell you why I call you that."

"It must be some horrible reason," she said with resignation, sitting down.

"I'm not a bad man," he said, towering over her as he moved to the side of her chair. "I just don't like opportunists."

Her eyes searched his blue ones. "Or women."

His face hardened. As he took a long drink from the glass he studied her quietly.

For an instant the room seemed to vanish—everything seemed to stand still. She found unexpected depths in those eyes of ice blue and her heart felt jumpy and odd. His lean, dark fingers caressed the glass he was holding, and she felt as if he were touching her. There was something fierce about the way he was looking at her; an odd kind of violence lingered under his thick black lashes. She had to struggle not to remember what they'd shared in that kitchen at Al's house.

"Is Sabina your real name?" he asked quietly.

"Yes." She looked back helplessly, locked to him by a gaze she was powerless to break, while her breath became ragged in her throat.

"Do you know who the Sabines were?" he continued in a voice like velvet.

She did, but she couldn't think; she felt hypnotized.

He bent, moving one hand to her throat. His fingers were cold, and she jumped.

"I won't hurt you," he whispered, misunderstanding the involuntary reaction. His fingers traced the wildly throbbing artery at her throat, and his mouth was so close she could taste the scent of whiskey on it. It should have revolted her, but it didn't. Her eyes fell to his hard lips, and she remembered with aching clarity the way they'd felt when he'd kissed her.

"The Sabines," he continued huskily, "were women taken by the Romans."

"Ra...raped by the Romans," she corrected. Her voice sounded odd.

"Sometimes men and women enjoy wild lovemaking," he whispered. "Passion in itself is violent. Like the way I feel with you, tulip, when I touch you and feel you start to tremble. The way you're trembling now. You want my mouth like hell, don't you?''

She wanted to deny it, to rail at him. But she couldn't even speak. Her lips were parted and she wanted his. Wanted his!

''I want yours, too,'' he whispered roughly, and the hand at her throat slid down to her collarbone, tracing exquisite patterns on her creamy skin. ''I want to touch you in ways that would shock you. My skin on yours, my mouth on your body…''

''Don't,'' she moaned, and her gray eyes, wider than saucers, looked up into his. ''I'm…I'm Al's girl.''

His nose nuzzled hers and his mouth threatened to come down and take possession of her lips. She could almost feel its texture, exciting, hungry. ''Then why,'' he whispered, ''are you begging me to kiss you?''

''Damn you!'' she whimpered, swatting at him.

He stood up with a mocking smile on his dark face, his eyes sparkling as they met hers. ''You fascinate me, Miss Cane,'' he said after a minute, fingering his whiskey glass idly as he studied her flushed face. "All that delicious innocence, waiting to be taken. Why hasn't Al had you? Are you afraid of sex?"

She was hardly able to catch her breath. Why did he affect her this way? "You have…a dirty mouth," she muttered, hating that faint amusement in his eyes.

"Yours is incredibly tempting, rock star," he replied, lifting his glass to his lips. "I'd like nothing more than to seduce you, right where you're sitting."

She started to jump at him, out of sheer frustrated fury, when another voice broke the silence.

"Where is everybody?" Al called from the hall. He sauntered in, oblivious of the tense undercurrents in the room. He was wearing a casual denim suit with a patterned blue shirt. It suited his fairness. But he wasn't any match for Thorn.

"You two look so different," Sabina observed quietly, glancing from one to the other.

"Our father was dark-headed and blue-eyed," Al explained. "And our mother was brunette and green-eyed. I guess we got the best of them both.''

Thorn's face hardened. "Let's go in," he said, gulping down the rest of his drink. He set the glass down roughly on the desk and strode out ahead of them.

"Ouch," Al muttered, hanging behind. "I never know which way he's going to jump. He and Mother must have really had it out over the phone the other night."

"Don't they get along at all?" Sabina asked.

"Once or twice a year." He led her into the dining room. "Let's eat. I'm famished!"

It didn't help that Thorn kept watching her at the dinner table. He had a predatory look in his eyes, and a rigid cast to his features that was disturbing.

"How did you become a rock star, Miss Cane?" he asked over dessert.

She flinched at the unexpected question. "Well," she faltered, fork poised over the delicious cake Juan had just served them, "I sort of fell into it, I suppose."

His straight nose lifted. "How?"

"I was told that I had a voice with potential," she said. "I tried out in an amateur com-

petition, where the prize was a one-night appearance at a downtown club. I won.'' She
shook her head and smiled wistfully. ''I was
delirious. I'd been waiting on tables up until
then, because it was the only work I could find.
I did the one-nighter, and the club management
liked me enough to keep me on. From there, I
got other engagements. Then I met up with The
Bricks and Sand Band.''

''Jessie told me about that,'' Al added. ''It
wasn't so much a meeting as a head-on colli-
sion.''

''Ricky Turner and the boys were hired to
play for me the first night at a rather sleazy
little joint off Bourbon Street,'' she said, her
eyes twinkling. ''Somehow, they'd gotten the
idea that I was a stripper instead of a singer,
and the drummer made a remark that set me
off the wrong way.'' She shrugged and took a
deep breath. ''Well, to make a long story short,
I knocked him into his base drum five minutes
before the performance.''

Thorn's mouth curled up reluctantly. ''But
you still teamed up?''

''We didn't have a choice that night.'' She
shook her head. ''Ricky laughed himself sick.

The drummer had quite a reputation. We did several numbers, and we seemed to score big with the audience. The manager suggested that we stay on for a few more nights. His business boomed. So Ricky and the guys and I decided to team up.'' She smothered a laugh. ''To this day the drummer still avoids me, but now we've got more offers than we can accept.''

She didn't tell him that she was trained to sing opera, or that she'd gone hungry a time or two to afford the lessons. Or that all the doors to the Met were closed by her dwindling finances. Or that the amateur competition she'd won had been won with an operatic aria. When the nightclub offer came, it was for quite a sum of money and she'd needed it too much to refuse. She thought about that $20,000 check Thorn had written out so carelessly and could have cried. It was nothing to him, but at one time that much money would have been her mother's salvation.

''Hey, you're a million miles away,'' Al teased.

''Sorry,'' she said, forcing a smile as she finished her dessert.

Thorn was still watching her from his kingly

position at the head of the table. She couldn't look at him. The luxury of letting her hungry eyes feast on his handsome features was too tempting. It made her remember how she'd felt when he'd kissed her. She'd been shocked by her wild response to him. He appealed to her senses in delicious ways. But he was the enemy, and she'd do well to remember it.

"Our mother also performs on stage," Al volunteered, ignoring Thorn's glare. "She does character parts. Right now she's doing a play in London."

Thorn set his cup down hard. "Al, I'd like to discuss that new field we're considering."

Al's eyebrows shot up. "You couldn't possibly be asking my opinion," he chided. "You never have before; you always go ahead and do what you please."

"You're coming into your majority next year," Thorn reminded. "It's time you took part in board decisions."

"My God, I'll faint," Al said with a little sarcasm. His eyes narrowed as he studied the older man. "Are you serious?"

"Always," Thorn said, with a pointed glance at Sabina. "In every way."

He was reminding her that he'd warned her off Al. She lifted her cup in a mock salute and smiled at him challengingly.

"Let's go," Thorn told his brother, rising. "You'll excuse us, Miss Cane? I'm sure you can find something with which to amuse yourself."

She glared at his broad back as he led Al into the study and closed the door firmly.

Old Juan, the man who kept house for Thorn, came to clear the table, and she offered to help. He smiled and shook his head. "No, *señorita*, but *muchas gracias*," he said charmingly. "Such work is not fit for such dainty hands. I will bring coffee and brandy to the living room, if you care to wait there."

"Thank you," she said, smiling at the dark little man. She'd expected Thorn to have an older woman doing the cooking and cleaning, but it seemed he didn't like any women around him. He had definite prejudices in that direction.

She wandered into the living room and stopped in the doorway to feast her eyes on the interior design. Like the den, it mirrored the personality of its owner. It was done in browns and tans with a burgundy leather couch and love seat and big sprawling armchairs in desert patterns. There was a huge Oriental rug by the ornate fireplace. Over the mantel was a portrait of a Hereford bull. On a nearby antique table stood an elegant chessboard and hand-painted wooden chess pieces. The drapes echoed the color schemes of the furniture, dark colors that gave the room a bold, masculine atmosphere.

There was a piano beyond the chessboard, a Baldwin. Sabina was drawn to it irresistibly. She sat down on the bench, her back straight, and raised the lid over the ebony and ivory keys. There had been a piano at the orphanage, and one of the matrons had taught her painstakingly how to play it, taking pity on her fascination with the instrument. Her fingers touched the keys, trembling with wonder at its exquisite tone.

Slowly, softly, she began to play Rachmaninoff's Second Piano Concerto, a passionate piece of music that mirrored her own confused emotions. Her eyes closed as her fingers caressed the cool keys, and she drifted away in a cloud of music.

She wasn't sure exactly when she became

aware of eyes watching her. She stopped in the middle of a bar and stared nervously toward the doorway where Thorn was completely still, spellbound, with Al at his shoulder.

"Don't stop," Thorn said quietly. He moved into the room and sat down on the sofa with a cigarette in his hand, motioning Al into a chair. "Please," he added gently.

Distracted, it took her a minute to pick up where she'd left off. Thorn's penetrating gaze made her nervous. But, as usual, the music swept her away, just as it did when she sang. She finished the piece with a flourish, closed the lid and stood up.

"You play brilliantly," Thorn said, and the words seemed to be forced. "Where did you learn?"

"I was taught by a friend," she said, neglecting to add whom or where. "She wasn't a professional, but she read music quite well. She taught me to sight read."

"She did a brilliant job," he said. "You could play professionally."

"No, thanks," she said with a nervous laugh. "It's too wearing. At least when I sing, I don't have to worry about where my hands are going. On the piano I'd do nothing but make mistakes in front of an audience." She sat down on the arm of Al's chair. "Do you play?" she asked him.

"No. Thorn does."

Surprised, she looked at the older man.

"Shocked?" he taunted, taking a draw from the cigarette. "I enjoy music. Not, however, that noise that passes for it in your world."

It was a challenge. He didn't like her ability; it irked him that she didn't fit the mold he was trying to force her into. Now he was going to cut back; his eyes told her so.

"Noise is a matter of taste," she told him. "I like rhythm."

He lifted an eyebrow and an amused smile turned up his hard, chiseled lips.

She stood up. Well, she might as well live down to the image he had of her. "Say, what do people do for amusement out here?" she asked Al.

"We watch movies," Al told her with a chuckle. "Thorn, want to join us?"

Thorn shook his head. "I've got some paperwork to get through."

Al led Sabina out of the room and down the

hall to another, smaller room. "We've got all the latest movies. Which would you like to see?" he asked, showing her the collection stowed beneath the VCR's giant screen.

"I'd really like to sit on the porch and listen to the crickets, if you want to know," she confessed. "But that would bother your brother. He likes me to run true to form."

He ruffled her hair. "Don't let him get to you. Thorn's crafty."

"So am I," she said. "Why does he dislike me so?"

"I think perhaps you remind him of our mother," he said slowly. "She's very much like you, in temperament. Though not in appearance. And there's something else... He really doesn't know how to handle his own emotions, so he pretends not to feel them. You get under his skin. I've never seen him like this."

"Maybe I ought to leave," she suggested hopefully.

"Not yet," he said with a twinkle in his eyes. "Things are just getting interesting."

"You won't leave me alone with him?" she blurted out.

He frowned. "Afraid of him?"

"Yes," she confessed.

"That's a first."

"I suppose it is," she said on a sigh. "He really gets to me, Al."

"Has he threatened you?" he asked suddenly.

Not wanting to alarm him, she laughed off his question. "In a way. But I'm not worried."

"I think I am," Al said quietly. "There's a very real hunger in his eyes when he looks at you. I've never seen exactly that expression in them before. He's crafty. Don't let him too close."

"Never mind about me," she reassured him. "I like a challenge. He is a sporting enemy, you know."

"You're incorrigible."

"Not to mention stupid," she teased. "Enough of that. You said you were going to manage some time with Jess. How?" she asked with a wry smile. "He's very sharp. If you invite her here—"

"Yes, I know," he said, checking his watch. "But if he thinks that you and I are watching a movie together, he'll be busy elsewhere, won't he?" he asked with a grin.

"Genius," she said, laughing. "But won't he hear the car?"

"No. Because I won't be driving it. Jessica's going to meet me about a quarter of a mile down the road. When the movie ends," he added, putting in the videocassette, "just go straight upstairs. I don't imagine Thorn will come out of his study for hours yet."

"What if he does? Or if the phone rings for you?"

"Tell him I've gone to the bathroom, and you'll give me the message when I come out," he said, gesturing toward the bathroom in the corner.

"Have it all figured out, hmm?" she teased.

"You have to, around Thorn. Sabina, I'll never be able to pay you back for this," he said gratefully.

She stood on tiptoe and brushed his cheek with her mouth, just as the door swung open and Thorn glared at them. He was wearing a tweed jacket with a white sweater and tan slacks, and looking irritated.

"I have to go to the office for an hour or so," he told his brother impatiently.

"I'll take messages while you're gone," Al promised, struggling not to show his relief.

Thorn glanced from Al to Sabina, and closed the door with a muffled slam.

"He hates it." He chuckled. "He hates the whole idea of my not marrying the oil refinery heiress. Well, I'm off. Hold down the fort!"

"Beat him back home. Please," she pleaded.

"Just go to bed and lock your door, and yell through it if he asks where I am," he said. "Tell him I ran out for coffee or back to my house to pick up something."

"Okay. Have fun."

He lifted an eyebrow. "Never fear."

He darted out the door and she sat down, glancing with no interest whatsoever at the screen. Halfway through the movie she cut the machine off, deciding she needed some fresh air. Borrowing a jacket from the hall, she walked out onto the porch.

The ranch was quiet amid the dark, peaceful night. She sat down in one of the oversized rocking chairs and the wicker squeaked pleasantly as she lazily nudged it into motion. She almost went to sleep, drinking in the night sounds, the distant baying of dogs, the singing of crickets. The stars were out and it was a perfect night for lovers. She was glad for Jessica that Al had finally admitted his feelings. She only hoped that they could all keep Thorn in the dark. Of course, once Jessica and Al were married, it would be too late. Thorn would have to accept Jess then.

So this was the oil baron's world. Classical music and quiet nights and open country. He wasn't really the sophisticated cynic she'd first met. She wondered if he'd ever really given in to his emotions, if he'd ever been in love. But that kind of thinking was dangerous, so she let her mind wander, lulled by the sounds of the countryside.

The soft purr of an engine startled her. She peered out ito the darkness, trying to see who it was. Al should be coming back any minute. But what if it wasn't Al?

She stood up just as Thorn appeared, taking the steps two at a time. He stopped at the post when he spotted her, his face scowling in the scant light from the windows.

"What are you doing out here alone?" he asked curtly. "Where's Al?"

"He had to run back to town to turn off something at his house."

"What?"

"He didn't say," she returned, fighting to keep calm.

"And he left you here all by yourself, songbird? How thoughtless. Why didn't he carry you off with him?"

She held on to the porch railing to keep from giving over to panic. "I didn't want to ruin his reputation," she said with a coy grin.

"You're engaged, for God's sake," he replied, coming closer. "Aren't you?"

"You were the one who had palpitations at the thought that we might want to share a room," she reminded him.

"I'm old-fashioned that way," he replied, his eyes glittering down at her.

"A strange attitude for a womanizer," she challenged.

He stood looking down at her, not speaking, not moving, and she realized belatedly that they were alone and he was the enemy.

"Family is different," he said after a few moments. "Family matters."

"Which is why you don't want me to belong to it."

"There's no question about your belonging to it, honey. No way am I going to let Al be hooked into marriage with a notorious..."

"Don't you dare call me foul names!" she warned. "I hit you once and I'll do it again. You really know nothing about me," she added.

His blue eyes narrowed. "What do you see in Al?" he asked bluntly.

She shrugged, dropping her eyes. She was still wearing the borrowed, oversized jacket, and her hair was blowing in the chill breeze. "He's gentle," she said finally.

Before she realized what was happening Thorn was looming over her. The dim light from the house cast a strange sheen in his eyes. "I frighten you, don't I?" he asked quietly.

"Yes." She'd never made a habit of lying. Except with that "engagement" to Al, and it was in a good cause.

"Why?" he persisted.

She smiled slowly. Ironic how safe she felt with him, even as her blood raced and her heart pounded and her legs trembled. She was afraid of everything and nothing when he was near. "I don't know," she admitted. "You wouldn't be a reincarnated ax murderer, by any chance?"

His hard mouth softened into a faint smile. "I hate it when you do that," he remarked. "I'm not used to quick-witted women."

"You aren't used to people, are you?" she asked gently. "I mean, you work with them, and you go to board meetings, and there are social obligations. But you keep to yourself, I think."

"I get the same impression about you," he said warily. He leaned against the post and studied her. "A pity you're wrapped up in ribbon and wearing a tag with Al's name on it. I might have given you a run for that money you want so badly."

"Why do you go around with women you have to buy?" she asked bluntly. This man was so different from her stereotyped impression of a rich man. He was hard and cold, but he would never have raised a hand to a woman. She knew that instinctively.

His eyes searched hers. "They don't get very close that way, Sabina," he said quietly.

Watching him light a cigarette she tugged the jacket closer. "I don't know whose this is," she said. "But I didn't want to go all the way upstairs to get my own…"

"It's mine," he said. "I don't mind."

She felt strange wearing it now, though, and she tingled at the thought of it lying against his hard body.

"How old are you, tulip?" he asked.

"Twenty-two," she returned. "Not quite young enough to be your daughter."

"No, not quite," he agreed with a lazy smile. "I was fourteen, my first time."

"Off with an older woman, I'll bet," she murmured demurely.

"She was an old lady of eighteen," he said, his eyes twinkling as she met his gaze. "The most sought-after girl in the school. When my father found out I got a whipping I'll never forget," he recalled. "My father had strong views on morality, and the fact that I was male didn't make one bit of difference to him."

"He didn't want his son to get a reputation for being easy," she teased. The smile faded then as she looked at him, wanting so much to ask about his parents.

"Yes, my mother loved him," he said quietly, reading the question. "But he was a hard man, Sabina. It wasn't easy for him to love. He thought of it as a weakness. In some ways, I can understand how my mother felt. She was a butterfly, always in the thick of society. He was like me. He much preferred the ranch to the city. They were basically incompatible. But that doesn't excuse her actions. He'd be alive today if she'd been faithful to him."

She was remembering her own mother, the pain of each new man, the horrible night when it all ended....

"What was your mother like?" he asked.

"Like yours," she said under her breath. She looked away, pulling the jacket closer. "I don't talk about her, to anyone."

He lit a cigarette. "Is she why you're still a virgin?"

She nodded. "I don't want that kind of life."

"Are you as passionate with Al as you were with me that night in the kitchen?"

The question startled her. She turned, searching for words. Good heavens, Al had never kissed her at all. She was still trying to come up with some kind of answer when he abruptly tossed the cigarette off the porch and moved toward her.

"No," she said, backing away. "No, Thorn, don't."

"You make my name sound like a benediction," he said in a hot breath. His hands shot out, lean, hurting hands, jerking her against his long, warm body, holding her there even as she struggled. "No, honey," he said in a voice like velvet, stilling her hips. "Don't do that."

She looked up, her hands flat against his chest, her eyes wild, her hair all over her face. "It isn't fair to Al," she said.

"Don't you think I know that?" he said in a grating voice. His eyes were glittering, his face as rigid as steel. His breath came heavily and hard. "I want you," he said huskily. He studied her breasts under the jacket, where they rose and fell with her uneasy breaths. "Are you wearing anything under that top?" he whispered.

"No," she said in a choked whisper. "I'm not."

She felt her knees go weak. Her eyes looked into his and she was lost. Drowning. Her body felt the warmth and power of his. Involuntarily,

GET 2 BOOKS FREE!

MIRA™

MIRA BOOKS, the brightest stars in women's fiction™, presents

the **Best** *of the* **Best**™

Superb collector's editions of the very best novels by the world's best-known authors!

* **Free Books!**   To introduce you to "The Best of the Best" we'll send you 2 books ABSOLUTELY FREE!

* **Free Gift!**   Get a stylish picture frame absolutely free!

* **Best Books!**   "The Best of the Best" brings you the best books by the world's hottest authors!

GET 2

HOW TO GET YOUR
2 FREE BOOKS AND FREE GIFT

1. Peel off MIRA sticker from front cover. Place it in space provided at right. This automatically entitles you to receive two free books and a lovely picture frame decorated with celestial designs.

2. Send back this card and you'll get 2 "The Best of the Best"™ novels. These books have a combined cover price of $11.00 or more but they are yours to keep absolutely free.

3. There's no catch. You're under no obligation to buy anything. We charge nothing – ZERO – for your first shipment. And you don't have to make any minimum number of purchases – not even one!

4. We call this line "The Best of the Best" because each month you'll receive the best books by the world's hottest authors. These are authors whose names show up time and time again on all the major bestseller lists and whose books sell out as soon as they hit the stores. You'll love getting them conveniently delivered to your home… and you'll love our discount prices.

5. We hope that after receiving your free books you'll want to remain a subscriber. But the choice is yours – to continue or cancel, anytime at all! So why not take us up on our invitation, with no risk of any kind. You'll be glad you did!

6. And remember…we'll send you a stylish picture frame ABSOLUTELY FREE just for giving "The Best of the Best" a try!

SPECIAL FREE GIFT!
We'll send you this lovely picture frame, decorated with celestial designs, absolutely FREE, simply for accepting our no-risk offer!

BOOKS FREE!

THE BEST OF THE BEST™: HERE'S HOW IT WORKS

Accepting free books places you under no obligation to buy anything. You may keep the books and gift and return the shipping statement marked "cancel." If you do not cancel, about a month later we will send you 3 additional novels and bill you just $4.24 each, plus 25¢ delivery per book and applicable sales tax, if any.* That's the complete price — and compared to cover prices of $5.50 each — quite a bargain! You may cancel at any time, but if you choose to continue, every month we'll send you 3 more books, which you may either purchase at the discount price...or return to us and cancel your subscription.

*Terms and prices subject to change without notice. Sales tax applicable in N.Y.

If offer card is missing write to: The Best of the Best, 3010 Walden Ave., P.O. Box 1867, Buffalo, NY 14240-1867

BUSINESS REPLY MAIL
FIRST-CLASS MAIL   PERMIT NO. 717   BUFFALO, NY

POSTAGE WILL BE PAID BY ADDRESSEE

THE BEST OF THE BEST
3010 WALDEN AVE
PO BOX 1867
BUFFALO NY 14240-9952

NO POSTAGE
NECESSARY
IF MAILED
IN THE
UNITED STATES

she brushed against him. Her full lips parted, wanting his mouth.

"I could touch you there," he murmured softly. His lips touched her forehead, open and moist as his hands slid around to her waist.

She trembled as his fingers pressed against her soft skin.

"Has he?" he asked curtly. "Has Al touched you there?"

She swallowed. "He... I'm old-fashioned, too. I've never..."

His mouth moved to her closed eyelids; his tongue tested the length of her lashes. "Untouched," he whispered deeply. "Soft and moon-kissed, and I want you so much, tulip. I've paid for women most of my life, in one way or another. But I've never been the first man." His breath sounded ragged, and the mouth hovering above hers was hard and warm and smoky. His hands were on her rib cage now, and she trembled as the tips of his fingers just brushed the outside edge of her taut breasts.

"This is just the beginning, this hunger. It gets worse." He breathed against her mouth. "I never gave a damn before, but I'm deliberately going to rouse you. I want to watch you. I want to hear those first sweet little gasps of passion when I touch you where no man ever has.''

"Thorn..." Her voice broke. She was trembling all over; her hands were buried in his soft white shirt, crumpling it over the wall of his chest. Her eyes were lost in his, and she was more helpless than she'd ever been in her life, completely at his mercy.

He lowered his head, his open mouth touching hers, brushing it with gentle probes that made her own lips part eagerly, so that he could fit them exactly to his.

He was so slow with her, so lazily confident, that she never thought of holding back. His warm, expert mouth pressed her lips apart and his tongue eased inside her mouth, tasting her with a rhythm that built and built and built as his fingers trespassed teasingly under her arms. The smell and feel and touch of him tormented her until finally her breath caught and she moaned, deep in her throat.

He felt her body arch against his thighs and he shifted his dark head to look down at her, at the mouth his had crushed and cherished.

Her eyes were wild, shocked, glazed with desire.

"If I touched you now, you'd cry out," he whispered, searching her flushed face.

"Please," she pleaded, hurting, aching for his hands.

"Is it really that bad?" he breathed deeply, fascinated by the expression in her soft eyes. "All right, baby, I'm going to give you what you want."

"So...hungry," she whispered tearfully. "Never...never before..."

"I know," he murmured. His mouth touched her eyelids, closing them. "Shhh. Be still, and I'll be so gentle with you...."

His hands were edging under her camisole top while his mouth threatened hers, poised over it. He found the hem and his warm hands slid up her rib cage, slowly, tenderly.

Her body jerked, trying to lift into his hands, but she was trembling like a leaf.

"Sweet," he whispered, shaken by her ardent response. "Oh, God, how sweet! Here, little one..."

He gave her his hands, and she did cry out, a sound that stunned him, shocked him. She threw her head back, her hands pressing against him, her body arching toward him in glorious abandon as waves of pleasure exploded in every cell of her body. His hands were warm and hard and callused, and when they contracted, she almost fainted.

"Thorn," she moaned. "Thorn, it's like fire; it burns, it burns," she whispered.

"God," he breathed reverently, shaken. She was like rose petals in his hands, so soft, so delicate, the skin smooth and warm, the tips hard in his palms. The first time... He took her mouth under his and felt his lips tremble as he kissed her and kissed her and kissed her. He was so far gone that the distant drone of a car only barely got through to him. She smelled of gardenias and his body was in agony with its need of hers.

He lifted his head. Her eyes opened, drowsy with passion, hungry for him. Her mouth... He had to brush it with his, just once more, to savor the honey of her lips.

"It's Al," he said unsteadily. He took a deep, steadying breath and didn't let go of her right away, because she looked weak enough to fold up. "You're a miracle," he whispered.

"A miracle. And you're his damn you! Damn you, Sabina!" Crushing her arms under his fingers as the car came closer, he pushed her roughly away and went into the house without another word.

She couldn't face Al, not like this. She ran into the house and down the hall and back into the VCR screening room. Hurriedly, she shoved the tape into the machine and fell into a chair. By the time Al walked in, she'd just barely gotten her nerves steady and her hair smoothed. She didn't want him asking questions. She couldn't have borne having to answer them right now. She was devastated.

"How did it go?" Al asked, sneaking in the room.

"He came back unexpectedly. I couldn't think fast enough. I told him you'd forgotten to turn off something at your house."

"Good girl! So he won't even be suspicious. That was quick thinking." He grinned. "Any problems?"

She shook her head, avoiding his eyes. "Of course not. Well, good night. See you in the morning."

"We'll go riding. At least, it will look that

way," he said with a chuckle. "I'm sneaking off one more time, to get the license."

"I'll be a nervous wreck!" she exclaimed, then rushed off without elaborating.

Behind the door of her bedroom, she collapsed. How had Thorn conquered her so easily? If Al hadn't come back... She blushed wildly, hotly, at the thought of where they were headed. She'd wanted him and it had been obvious that he wanted her, too. Her body still pulsed with the pleasure his hands had taught her. Her mouth burned from his kisses. She felt an ache that wouldn't stop. Tears welled up in her eyes. Oh, Jessica, she thought. If you only knew what I'm going through for you!

She turned out the light and went to bed, hoping the days would pass quickly. She was far too vulnerable to Thorn, and she was dubious about her dwindling strength. He could put her in an impossible situation. And what then? What if he went too far and seduced her? He'd promised he wouldn't, but he'd lost control. She'd felt it. He wanted her just as fiercely as she wanted him, and it could happen. That would destroy her. It would ruin her future. Because there could never be another man after Thorn. Never.

Chapter Five

Tugging on a pair of gray slacks with a pull-over V-necked striped top and boots, Sabina went downstairs the next morning, expecting to find Al at the breakfast table. Instead, she found only Thorn.

He was sitting at the head of the table, toying with a napkin, obviously waiting for something or someone. He was in denim today, rugged looking, a cowboy from out of the past. His shirt was half open in front, and she could see dark skin and a feathering of body hair. She remembered her own voice pleading with him to touch her. Her face flamed, her heartbeat shook her. She wanted to run.

His blue eyes jerked up and he found her watching him. "Sit down, songbird. Juan's just bringing breakfast."

There was no way out. She pulled out the chair next to his and sagged into it, turning over the cup in her saucer as Thorn poured hot coffee into it from the carafe.

"Cream or sugar?" he asked.

"I take it black," she said. "Caffeine keeps me going on tour. But I've never had the luxury of cream and sugar."

His eyes wandered over her shoulders, her bare arms. "Is that how you stay so thin?"

"I'm not a heavy eater," she said. Her eyes focused on the coffee cup, until he reached out unexpectedly and tilted her chin up to his probing stare.

"It isn't fair to Al," he said quietly.

"What isn't?" she stammered.

"Wearing that," he said, indicating the engagement ring flashing in the overhead light. "Not when you can want another man the way you wanted me last night."

"I did not—" she began defensively.

"Don't." He touched her mouth with a lean forefinger, and his eyes were stern and narrow.

"Don't lie. I could have taken you if he'd waited another half hour to come home."

"Leave me alone, Thorn!" she burst out.

"I won't," he promised. He leaned back in his chair and lit a cigarette. "I can't. You won't take advice. So you can take the consequences."

"What are they?" she returned. "A night in your bed?"

"I'd love that," he said with genuine feeling as his eyes wandered hungrily over her face and made her flush with embarrassment. "It's been a long time since I've wanted a woman the way I want you."

"I'm not like that," she said with quiet pride.

"Yes. That makes it worse." He sipped his coffee. "Where are you from, Sabina?"

"New Orleans. Why?"

"How did you meet Al?"

"Jessica introduced us."

He shot her a piercing look. "Nice girl, Jessica. Did you know that she's in love with my brother?"

Her cheeks burned and the cup almost overturned in her hands.

"I see that you do," he persisted, leaning forward to flick ashes in the ashtray. "Doesn't it bother you, hurting her?"

"What do you care about Jessica's feelings? I didn't think secretaries mattered in your world."

"I don't like that," he said coldly, and his icy, pale blue eyes glittered. "I'm no snob, songbird."

"Oh, but you are, Mr. Thorndon," she assured him bitterly. "You have deep prejudices."

"Only about a certain type of woman, which has nothing whatsoever to do with breeding," he returned.

"Breeding," she scoffed. Her eyes lit up. "You'd probably just as soon breed people the way you breed bulls. You keep a portrait of a Hereford bull over your living-room mantel, but I don't see any pictures of loved ones on your walls. Don't people count with you, oil baron?"

His jaw tightened as he crushed out the cigarette. "You never will, honey," he said in a voice as smooth as silk. "Physically, maybe, but no other way."

"Thank God," she replied fervently.

His temper flared, but at that moment Al chose to join them at the table.

"Morning," he said with an ear-to-ear grin. "Breakfast ready?"

"Juan!" Thorn roared, his voice deep and piercing.

"*Si, señor,* I bring it now!" came the quick reply from the kitchen.

"When Thorn growls, everybody jumps," Sabina murmured dryly, with a pointed glance in Thorn's direction.

"You may learn how, before it's over," he warned her.

"You two aren't arguing, are you?" Al asked Thorn. "Future in-laws ought to get along."

If looks could kill, Al would have dropped dead from the impact of Thorn's angry glare.

"Don't listen for wedding bells too soon, brother," he warned Al. "There's plenty of time. You're young."

"Who made you wait?" Al asked him with a calculating stare. "Remember that stacked blonde you wanted to marry, and Dad threatened to disinherit you? You ran off with her, but he followed and propositioned her, right in front of your eyes. He told her that you wouldn't inherit anything if you married her, but that he had plenty of money, and she switched loyalties on the spot. Is that why you're so worried about me making the same mistake?''

"Go to hell," Thorn said softly. He got up from the table and walked off without a backward glance.

"How horrible," Sabina said under her breath. Her heart ached when she considered the pain Thorn must have endured at such a young age.

"Yes, it was, but he's let it lock him up for life," Al said quietly. "He's hardly human these days, all because of one woman who betrayed his trust. He's got to stop living in the past.''

"He'll get even," she said.

He smiled softly. "Not in time," he promised. "Not nearly in time. Let's eat and we'll hit the trail."

They rode so far the ranch was out of sight. Thorn hadn't been seen since breakfast, and Sabina felt oddly sad that he'd gone without it.

He must be starving. When they reached the fork in the trail, Al waved and rode on ahead. They'd agreed that if Thorn came looking, she'd say Al had decided to give his roan a workout and didn't want to force her to ride so fast when she was out of practice. She rubbed her arms, wishing she'd borrowed a jacket. It would be cold until the sun rose higher in the sky.

She reined in at the river that cut through the property and sat quietly in the clearing, watching the water flow lazily downstream. She got down to examine a set of tracks, and grinned to herself. Deer tracks. They must have watered at the river. Her grandfather had taught her how to track deer; she'd never forgotten. She felt like one of the old pioneers.

"Are you lost, city girl?" came a sardonic drawl from behind her.

She glanced around, not even surprised to find Thorn leaning over the pommel of his own horse, watching her.

"Nope. I'm tracking deer," she informed him.

He swung down out of the saddle, tilting his wide-brimmed Stetson at a jaunty angle over his eyes, and knelt down beside her. His bat-wing chaps spread out and his boots made a leathery creak with the motion.

"Tracks," he exclaimed.

"Sure," she told him. "That one's a buck. It's got a pointed, cloven hoof. The other is a doe; it's rounded."

"Who taught you that?"

"My grandfather. He used to take me tracking every fall, before deer season opened," she confessed. "At least, until he died." Her eyes grew sad with the memory. "At that time he was the biggest thing in my life. I worshipped him."

"What else did he teach you?"

"Oh, little things. How to tell when rain was coming, how to make things grow. He was a farmer."

Thorn got to his feet slowly, staring down at her with a confused expression. "You worry me."

"Why?" she asked, rising gracefully. "Because I know how to track deer?"

"Because you don't fit any mold I've ever seen," he said, lifting his chin and scrutinizing her. "Because I want you. I could almost hate you for making me vulnerable, even physically."

That was a shocking admission, but it was like him. He didn't pull punches. She wouldn't have expected it. He was a hard man, and it would have been someone like him a hundred years ago who would have tamed this land where they were standing, and fought off hostile forces, and made the fields green and bountiful.

"You're staring again," he said sharply.

"You're very much a man, Mr. Thorndon," she said, spellbound enough to be honest with him. "I've never met anyone like you before. The men in my world are shallow people. You're solid and honest. I meant it when I said I'd have liked you for a friend."

"No, you wouldn't," he said with a mocking smile. "You'd have liked me for a lover, and that's what we'd be already if you hadn't tangled yourself up with my kid brother."

"I don't think so," she returned. "I'm afraid of you. You take people over, you own them. I couldn't bear to be owned."

"I could make you like it."

And probably he could, but she wouldn't let

herself think about that. Her gaze drifted beyond him, toward the meadow behind the banks that stretched to a long line of trees on the horizon.

"It's so lovely here," she said. "So quiet. How can you bear New Orleans after you've lived here?"

His jaw became taut. "I cope—with most things."

She turned back to her horse, but Thorn was in front of her before she got two steps, a solid wall she couldn't bypass.

"It's not that easy," he said, and his hard, lean hands caught her by the arms and held her in front of him. "Where's my brother?"

"He gave the roan its head. He'll be right back," she insisted.

"Not for a little while, Sabina," he whispered, leaning toward her. "Kiss me. I went to bed aching for you; I woke up hurting.... Kiss me, damn you!"

His mouth pressed into hers, and none of the teasing foreplay of the night before was left between them. He lifted her against his lean, powerful body and his arms swallowed her while his mouth taught her new lessons in the art of intimacy. Suddenly, she felt his body harden against her, enticing her. Protesting, she twisted and his hand swept down to the base of her spine to hold her still, even as a groan burst from his lips.

He lifted his head, and his eyes frightened her with their wild glitter.

"Don't move against me that way," he whispered hoarsely. "It arouses me unbearably."

She blushed, but he bent his head again, and his mouth stifled the words she was about to utter.

Her fingers let go of his shirt to slide under it. She sighed as she felt the curly hair covering his muscles, and her fingers tangled in it. She felt his body tauten even more and sensed that he was reacting to the gentle movement of her hands. Her education in sensual things was sadly behind that of most people; there'd been no one to ask except girlfriends, and most of them knew as little as she did.

"Sabina, for God's sake, don't, baby," he whispered, stilling her hands. He drew away slightly, looking more formidable than ever, his eyes glazed, his face taut.

She slid her hands out from under his shirt, shaken by the fierce ardor she'd provoked, and by her headlong response to it.

She could hardly breathe and Thorn's heart was pounding like a trip-hammer. He laughed softly, strangely, and his chest rose and fell in irregular jerks. "You burn me up," he said huskily. "The smell of you, the feel of you... It's been years since I felt like this."

His words were flattering, but she was getting nervous. They were in a deserted place, where no one would look for them, and Al wouldn't be back for hours. There was a wildness in Thorn that she hadn't expected at the beginning, a reckless passion that matched her own free spirit.

"Thorn," she whispered.

His mouth took the whisper and inhaled it, opening her soft lips to a deep, slow, probing kiss. His hands slid down her sides to her hips and drew them lazily against his in easy, dragging movements. She was so lost in the warm teasing of his mouth that she didn't protest this time. His body and its responses and demands were becoming familiar now. He was like a part of her already.

"I've never made love standing up," he whispered in a voice that was deep and a little unsteady. "You make me wonder how it would be."

A tiny wild sound escaped from her throat, and he smiled against her lips. "I want you," he growled softly. His hands slid to the backs of her thighs and lifted and pressed until she thought she'd go crazy with the sweet, piercing pleasure. He laughed again, roughly. "I want you. I want to lay you down in the grass and let my body melt into yours. But that would be playing right into your hands, wouldn't it, witch woman? You'd love that, making me lose my head with you. You'd hold it over me like a scimitar...."

"Thorn!" she exclaimed, dragging her mouth from his. "I'm not like that, I'm not!" Her drowsy eyes sought his and she searched their cool blue depths slowly, remembering all at once what Al had said over the breakfast table about the blonde who'd betrayed Thorn. Her fingers lifted to his mouth, touching it gently, liking the hard warmth of it. "She was crazy, wanting money instead of you...."

His eyes flashed. The whispered words

seemed to anger him. He caught her long hair and jerked her face up to his. "She was a tease, too," he said curtly. "A woman with an eye to the main chance."

The words came out like an insult, and she knew that whatever had been growing between them had wilted.

"You're hurting me," she said quietly.

His nostrils flared and his face hardened, but slowly he released his cruel hold on her hair and let her move away from him. His gaze went down to the small fingers still pressed against his chest, and he lifted them away.

He wasn't a man at the mercy of his emotions now, she thought, watching him light a cigarette with cool, steady hands. He'd become as cold as stone.

His mouth curled slowly. "You've got one hell of a lot of spirit. Al may miss you, after all."

"He isn't going anywhere."

"No. But you are." He lifted his head, studying her insolently. "I'm working on a little surprise for you, tulip. Just another day or so, and I'll have everything I need."

"How exciting," she murmured. "I can hardly wait. Does Al know?"

The smile faded. "I don't want him hurt any more than he has to be. Not that you seem to mind playing around with me behind his back."

How could she tell him that the engagement was a bogus one, that Thorn appealed to her senses in a way that left her completely at his mercy? That she loved him, wanted him, needed him. It was a maelstrom of discovery that left her knees weak. It couldn't happen so quickly, could it? He was arrogant and ruthless and narrow-minded. But he was more man, pound for pound, than any male she'd ever run across in her life. Her eyes coveted the very sight of him. And because of that, she turned away and wouldn't let him see her face again.

"I'll leave you to your work, oil baron," she said as she mounted her horse. "I'm going to find Al."

"Enjoy his company while you can," he returned, mounting his own horse with lazy grace. "You haven't got long."

"What was your father like, Thorn?" she asked suddenly, curious.

"Like me," he said shortly.

"No wonder your mother is the way she is," she said sadly. "She must have been devastated when he died."

He frowned. "What a hell of a way she has of showing it!"

"Al showed me a picture of your father; he's told me things about him." Her hand lifted to shade her eyes from the sun. "He must have been a strong man. There aren't a lot of strong men in the world. I imagine she's been looking all this time for someone who halfway measured up to him, without the least success. She's relatively young, Al said. What a pitiful way to live."

He glared at her, but he was listening. "She might have showed him she cared while he was still alive. He'd be alive, but for her."

Her soft eyes wandered all over him, loving every rippling muscle, even the stubborn set of his jaw. He'd changed her whole life so quickly. "Perhaps he made it impossible for her to show it. Perhaps she only wanted to capture his attention. And afterward, after it happened, the guilt would have been terrible. Some men take a lot of forgetting," she said.

"How the hell would you know?" he challenged.

He was back to his old impossible self. She shrugged delicately and rode away without answering. If she'd said anything else, she might as well be talking to the wind. She rode back to the path where she'd left Al, dismounted, and sat on a stump waiting for him to return.

She could hardly believe how fast it had happened. She hardly knew Thorn, for heaven's sake! But he'd worn on her nerves and her emotions and her heart more in the past few days than most men had in months, even years. She wanted him, and it was oddly comforting to realize that he felt the same hunger for her. It was a dead-end street, of course. There was no possible future in it. But while she could see him and be near him, she took a terrible pleasure in her growing love for him. There was a lot of man under that cruel, cynical exterior. She was only sorry he was her enemy, that he'd never let her see behind his mask. It would be sheer heaven to be loved by such a man.

Al appeared a few minutes later, grinning. "We got the license," he said, giddy with excitement. "And we decided to set the date. We're getting married the day after Easter."

"That's Monday!" Sabina exclaimed.

"Yes! Oh, God, I'm so happy," he burst out, and danced her around the clearing in a mad little waltz.

Sabina laughed and danced, and tried not to think of how soon her bubble was going to burst. When Al broke the news to Thorn, it would all be over, and she'd never see the oil baron again.

"How about the ring?" she exclaimed.

"You can give it back when we drive to New Orleans Monday morning," he explained. "We want you to come along and stand up with us at the service. Okay?"

"I'd love to! Jessica and you. It's been my fondest dream."

"Mine, too, but it wouldn't have been possible without your help," Al said solemnly. "Thorn would have stopped us. This is the only way it could have worked. Has he been at you again?"

"Not really. We just talked," she lied, crossing her fingers behind her back.

"Good." Al let her go and mounted his horse, watching her mount beside him.

"But I've made him mad again, I'm afraid."

"How?"

"I told him your mother must miss your father terribly and be looking for someone who measures up to him," she murmured.

"That's what I've always thought," he replied. "Dad was one of a kind."

"Like Thorn," she said involuntarily.

He studied her, frowning. "Sabina, don't lose your heart to him. He hasn't got one of his own."

"I know that already," she said. "Don't worry about me, I'll be fine. Besides, a few days from now, it will all be a memory." That was a sobering thought. "Hey, I'll race you back!"

"You're on!"

And they galloped back to the house.

Thorn went out that evening, resplendent in his evening wear, and Sabina felt a surge of mad jealousy as she imagined him with some slinky blonde like the one he'd brought to Al's party.

"He does draw women," Al muttered later as they watched television. "He always has. But not one of them touches him emotionally. He says he'll never let any woman have a hold on him."

"I imagine he must have reason, don't you?" she said. "Can I play the piano?"

"What? Sure!" He turned off the television. "If you don't mind, I'm going to take advantage of Thorn's absence and go call Jessica."

"Mind? Get out of here and do it! I'm delighted to have some time to myself. Not that you aren't good company," she added.

He chuckled. "Don't wear out the keys."

"Not me."

He left and she played late into the night, her fingers touching the keys that Thorn's fingers had touched. It was a wildly exhilarating thought, and made her hungrier than ever just for the sight of him. But when she finished and went to bed, he still hadn't come home.

He wasn't at breakfast, either, but Al looked disgruntled as they dug into the hearty egg and bacon platter that Juan had prepared.

"Thorn's having a party Saturday night," he muttered. "And he's invited Jessica."

"Uh, oh. Think he's suspicious?" she asked quickly.

"I don't know. He says the party is being held to announce our engagement. But it's all a rushed-up job, with telephoned invitations. And it's not like Thorn to give in so easily. I think we've been discreet enough, but he's made some long-distance calls, and I overheard something that worries me." Al lifted his head, and his eyes were narrow with concern. "Listen, what could he find out about you if he dug really deep?"

She stared at him blankly. Her mind whirled, grasping. No, she thought wildly, no he couldn't find out anything after all these years. "Well...not much," she faltered. "Why?"

"Because he's in a good mood this morning. And that makes me suspicious."

She glowered at her toast. "Maybe it was just good humor left over from his night out," she said.

Al looked at her long and hard, but he didn't say a word.

A visiting cattleman stopped by after lunch, and Al went to show him around the ranch while Thorn took care of business in his study. Sabina sneaked out the door and went around the back of the house into the woods, beyond the little gazebo that so beautifully matched the house and faced the distant pastures. It was an unseasonably warm day. In her jeans with a green knit top, she looked younger than ever, with her long and soft hair blowing in the wind.

Her mind drifted as she watched a bird circle and soar toward the top of a huge live oak near the small stream. She wished it was warm enough to paddle in the creek.

"You look like a wood nymph."

She whirled to find Thorn standing behind her. He was clad in a white shirt and dark blue slacks with a suede blazer, all sleek muscle and dark tan. A feathering of crisp, curling black hair peeked out of his shirt. He was wearing his wide-brimmed creamy Stetson, and he looked suave and very Western.

"I'm just getting some air," she said defensively.

"Why aren't you with your intended?" he asked, leaning back against a tall oak, his boot propped behind him, his arms folded.

"Al was talking business; I didn't think I'd be welcome."

"Al doesn't know anything about the cattle business," he said. "He's buying time with Bellamy until I get there." He smiled faintly as he studied her. "The longer I take, the more Bellamy will worry. By the time I get there, he'll sell at my price. That's business, tulip."

"You said you'd tell me why you called me tulip," she reminded him. He was almost approachable today. She even smiled at him.

"There's a song about a yellow tulip and a big red rose," he murmured.

The song was one her mother used to sing, and she knew the words quite well. It was an old song—and one of the lines was something about it being heaven "when you caressed me" and "your lips were sweeter than julep...." She stared at him and went as red as the rose in the song.

"I see you know the song," he remarked, smiling insolently.

"I'm engaged to Al," she told him.

"Give him back the ring."

"I can't," she growled.

"That's the last chance you'll get from me,"

he said, his face grim. ''You'd better take it, while you still can.''

''Is that a threat?'' she asked with a laugh.

''It's much more than a threat.'' He was looking at her as if he'd never seen her before, an odd expression in his blue eyes. ''You're unique, Sabina,'' he said. ''And if you hadn't proven to me already that you're just after Al's money, I might be tempted to forget everything else. But I can't stand by and let Al make this kind of mistake.''

''Are you going to spend your life running interference for him?'' she asked quietly, not making a challenge of it. ''He's twenty-four. Eventually he'll have to stand on his own. And what if you aren't there to prop him up?''

''You're missing the point,'' he said flatly. Tugging a cigarette out of his pocket, he lit it, inhaling deeply. ''I've spent the past ten years of my life building up the company. I've made sacrifices....'' He took a draw from the cigarette and let the smoke out roughly. ''I'm not going to let him throw away his inheritance. It was hard bought.''

She looked at him openly, seeing the lines of age in his face, the wear and tear on him.

"Al was fourteen when your father died," she recalled. "You had all the responsibility then, didn't you?"

For an instant he looked vulnerable. Then as if the shutters came down, his expression was masked. "I didn't break under it."

"I don't think you can be broken," she said, searching his eyes. "I even understand."

"Oh, yes, I'm sure you do," he said, eyes narrowing as he held her gaze. "Your own life hasn't been easy street until now, has it?"

He couldn't know, she assured herself. She shrugged. "What do you mean, until now?"

"Designer jeans," he remarked. "Designer gowns. Expensive coats. You live well for a struggling singer."

If only he knew! She smiled inwardly. "I do okay," she said.

"How many boyfriends have you had in your young life?" he asked.

Her shoulders rose and fell. "None, really," she admitted, letting her eyes fall to his shiny boots, oblivious of the momentary softening in his face. "Guess I never had much time for all that. I've worked all my life."

His jaw clenched. "Yes. So have I."

"Not like I have, rich man." She laughed, throwing back her dark head. All her tiny triumphs glittered in her eyes. "I've waited tables and scrubbed floors. I've worked double shifts and fended off roaming hands and smiled over the nastiest kinds of propositions. I've worked in clubs so rough they had two bouncers. And I've done it without any help at all, from anybody!"

He didn't speak. His firm lips closed around the butt of the cigarette as he took another draw and then crushed it under his boot. "Did you get tired of the climb up? Is that why you've decided to marry Al when you're not in love with him?" he asked bluntly.

"Why do you say that?" she stammered.

"You never touch each other." He moved away from the tree and loomed over her, tall and threatening and unbearably masculine. "You smile at him, but not with love. You don't even kiss him."

She shifted backward restlessly, and he followed, too close. "I'm not demonstrative in public," she insisted.

"You're not demonstrative in private either, are you?" he demanded. His hands shot out and suddenly drew her close, so that his breath was on her forehead and his body threatened hers from head to toe. Her heart seemed to stop beating at the unexpected proximity. "You even freeze up with me, until I start kissing you, tulip."

"Thorn, don't," she whispered.

"I can't help myself," he said on a hard, contemptuous laugh. "I can't stand within five feet of you without losing my head. Haven't you noticed? My God, I hate what you do to me!"

She looked up into his deepening blue eyes and shivered with apprehension. Could he sense the secret, dark pleasures that she felt from the tautening of his body against hers, from the crushing strength of the hands gripping her arms?

Around them came the sound of birds, and the faraway rippling of water in the creek. The wind was stirring the limbs of the trees, and leaves crunched underfoot as she shifted in his embrace. But she was more aware of her own heartbeat, of the fleeting nature of her time with him. Just a few more days... after that she'd never see him again, she knew it. Once

Al was safely married, the oil baron would put her out of his mind. This, all of this, was just a means to an end, an attempt to make her break the engagement. But she was getting involved in ways she'd never meant to. She looked at him and loved him, bad temper, ruthlessness and all.

"It will all be over soon," she said softly.

"Sooner than you realize," he replied sharply. "Break off the engagement, while you can. Don't make me hurt you. I don't really have any taste for it now. But I have to protect Al."

Involuntarily, her fingers reached up, hesitated, and then touched his thick, dark eyebrows. Incredibly, his eyes closed, he stood very still, not moving at all. And that response made her bold. She traced all the hard lines of his bronzed face, learning its patrician contours, touching high cheekbones, his straight nose, his broad forehead, the indentations in his cheeks, the firm, warm line of his lips, his jutting, stubborn chin. His breath stirred as her fingers lingered beside his mouth.

She felt an answering hunger. Was it so much to ask, just one more kiss? One more

passing of lips against hers? One kiss to remember to live on? She rose on tiptoe, her
hands behind his strong neck, and touched her
mouth to his chin. It was as high as she could
reach, but not nearly enough.

"Thorn," she breathed huskily. "Thorn,
please…"

He was breathing as roughly as she was.
"What do you want from me, Sabina?" he
whispered back.

"Memories," she managed to get out.

His eyes opened, dark and very soft. He
reached down and picked her up in his arms,
holding her while he searched her hungry eyes.
"Memories," he said gently, in a tone he'd
never used with her before. "Yes, I can give
you those. In another time, another place—I
could have given you a child as well."

She trembled, her eyes filling with tears, and
he buried his face against her throat as he carried her deeper into the woods.

"I want you," she told him, whispering it,
her voice torn with hunger and pain.

"Me, and not Al?" he asked.

She drew in a breath and looked up into his

eyes, wanting only to explain, to tell him everything. But she didn't dare.

His face hardened, even as his eyes blazed with open desire. He laid her down under a big oak tree, on a pallet of leaves, and slid alongside her. "I'm richer than Al is," he said under his breath. "If money is the big draw, why not set your sights on me, tulip?"

"It isn't money," she said hesitantly.

"Well, it damned sure isn't love," he shot at her. His eyes kindled as they wandered the length of her body and back again, hungry on her breasts, her lips, her face. "Beautiful," he whispered. "You're so beautiful you take my breath, my will, my mind. I hold you and want nothing more from life than the taste of your mouth on mine."

"We're enemies," she whispered sadly.

"If it weren't for Al, and your innocence, we'd be lovers," he said. He ran his hand slowly over her shoulder, her collarbone, holding her eyes as he slid it onto her breasts and traced the hard tips.

Her lips parted with the unexpected movement, and he bent and took the sound from them with his own. She closed her eyes and the kiss got harder, deeper, hungrier. She moaned. His breath came heavily. He moved a hand to his suede jacket, unbuttoned it, and tossed it aside. He opened his shirt and tugged it free of his trousers, and drew her hands against his hard, hair-feathered chest. His mouth became more demanding, and she felt herself getting weaker by the second, done in by her own consuming love for him, by the pleasure she'd never known before. She sighed, nuzzling her face against him while his warm, deft fingers made quick work of buttons and hooks, and suddenly smoothed over her with exquisite delicacy, petal-smooth, feather-warm.

She gave a high-pitched little cry and tried to curl up, but he eased her onto her back and smoothed the fabric completely away from her body.

The breath he took was audible as he stared down at cream and mauve contrasts, lifting gracefully with her sighs. ''Oh, God,'' he whispered reverently, poised over her.

Her wide, gray eyes searched the hardness of his face, looking for vulnerability, but it only grew harder as he looked at her. She could feel

a sudden, helpless reaction as he stared bla-
tantly at her breasts, and it embarrassed her.
She tried to cover them, but he brought her
hands to his mouth, shaking his head.

"Don't be shy," he said gently. "I'm just
as aroused as you are."

His eyes glittered as he suddenly moved
down, shifting so that his whole body covered
hers, with his elbows taking the brunt of his
formidable weight. "See?" he murmured as
his hips moved in a slow rotation against hers,
and she felt the blatant proof of the statement.
"My God, I want to take you," he said huskily. "I want to strip you and grind your body
into the leaves under mine, and make you cry
out when the moment comes...."

Her face felt hot. She pressed her fingertips
against his hard mouth as the pictures flashing
in her mind embarrassed her. "You...
mustn't."

"Watch," he whispered, drawing her eyes
down to his chest. He moved, shifting so the
thick hair over it teased her breasts. The abra-
sive contact shocked her with pleasure, and her
body suddenly jerked, arching helplessly

against his, while her eyes told him how helpless she was to stop it.

"Your mind may want to stop, but your
body can't. You want me. It may be pure in-
stinct, because we both know you've never
known the full intimacy of a man's body."

"I want to," she moaned, touching his chest
helplessly. "I don't care if it hurts, I want
you..."

"Sabina," he whispered. His mouth opened
on hers and he gave her the full weight of his
body, holding her, devouring her eager lips.
She whimpered, and the sound made him shudder. Her body trembled as the warmth and
strength of his burned into it, his chest pinning
her soft breasts, his legs tangling in hers.

His hand edged between her breasts, his
thumb stroking her, his fingers tracing her. His
breath quickened, and he suddenly shifted, his
mouth moving from hers down to one creamy
breast.

She cried out, arching, her body shuddering
with unbelievable pleasure, and her glazed eyes
met his as he lifted his head. His hand stroked
her, warm and confident and soothing.

"This is what passion is all about," he said

softly, holding her gaze. "Total, absolute loss of control. Sensual oblivion. A few minutes of this and you'd kill to have me end the torment."

Her eyes stared up into his, through a fog of hunger and need and love.

He sat up, holding her down by the waist, studying the visible tremor of her body. He was none too calm himself, but he fought for self-control. He sighed heavily then, smiling ruefully at the expression on her face.

His lean hands shook her gently. "Virgins are hell on the nervous system," he murmured.

Her mind was only beginning to focus. "I would have begged you," she said numbly.

"Yes. But even then I wouldn't have gone any further." He drew the front of her bra together and fastened it, then her blouse, with slow, steady hands. "A casual relationship isn't for you. I don't think it ever would be, despite the offer."

"Thank you," she whispered.

He studied her quietly. "Now tell me you're not really marrying Al."

Was that why he'd made love to her? she

wondered miserably. To make her break the engagement? Her eyes closed. "I still am."

He glared down at her with pure hatred. "You have until tomorrow night to give him back the ring. If you don't..."

She fumbled for words. "I'm sorry," she said. "I can't."

He got to his feet angrily, buttoning his shirt and snatching up his jacket and hat while she sat and watched him curiously.

"My God, you're something," he said. It was no compliment. He glared at her openly. "I've never known a woman to be so damned mercenary!"

That hurt, but she didn't let him see how much. "And you're as unprincipled yourself, oil baron," she shouted back. "You made love to me just to make me break the engagement, didn't you?"

His face went rock hard. "Sure," he said coldly. "I'm ruthless, remember? I thought you might be persuaded to settle for me."

"For how long?" she asked with a bitter laugh. "A few weeks, until you sated yourself?"

"That would depend on how much you

wanted," he said with deliberate cruelty, as if he knew! "Most women will sell themselves for the right price or the right reason."

Her face paled, and she could have sworn there were traces of regret in his expression. She turned away. "Thanks for the lessons."

"You're an apt pupil. But school's out now."

"Just as well," she said. "The tuition is too high."

"You're paying for experience," he said tauntingly.

Her head jerked around, her eyes revealing hatred for all the other women he'd had before her. "Did you pay them?" she asked.

His eyes narrowed. "Sure. A diamond here, a mink there. Trinkets."

Trinkets. The price of survival. Her eyes grew wild, her face blanched as she saw her mother's face at the end of life, heard the pitiful words come torturously out of that frail throat.

"Oh, damn you!" Sabina cried, hating him for being that kind of man, hating him for what others had done to her mother, for what they had made of her. "Damn you, damn you...!" She sobbed.

"Sabina, wait!" There was an odd hesitation in his deep voice when she turned and began to run. But she didn't stop. Instead she let the wind cut into her face, let the tears cloud her vision as she ran on, lost in her own hell of memories.

Chapter Six

After she washed her tear-stained face and calmed down, Sabina changed into a soft, clinging brown-and-cream dress that suited her dark hair and eyes. Gathering her courage, she smoothed her hair and went back downstairs. She'd purposefully taken her time, so that the Thorndon brothers and the visiting cattleman were just coming back into the house when she reappeared. She wouldn't look straight at Thorn; she couldn't. Instead she went to Al, who immediately gathered her to his side—a movement that Thorn watched with cynical eyes and a mocking smile.

"Want to ride over to Houston with us?" Al

asked her. "I'm going to show Mr. Bellamy the city on the way to the airport." He indicated the heavyset, smiling man nearby.

Sabina nodded.

"Take your time," Thorn told the two men, but his brooding gaze never left Sabina. "I've got a business meeting in New Orleans in an hour. I'll go alone."

Relieved, Sabina was glad of the opportunity to escape from Thorn's sensual pull, even for a little while. She went with Al and the cattleman and was delighted when the outing kept them away from the ranch until late that evening. By the time they got home, it was bedtime, and Sabina was only too glad to have avoided another confrontation. *Oh, Thorn,* she thought miserably, *why did it have to be this way?* Why couldn't they have met under different circumstances? He wanted her so much, there had to be a glimmer of feeling for her under all that ice. Perhaps he might even have loved her, if she'd had a chance to be herself with him. The one time they'd really talked, there had been a rare rapport between them. And in the woods, he'd whispered, "Another time and place, I might have given you a child...."

It reminded her of the taunt she'd made the first day at the ranch, about having babies, and Thorn's eyes had gone to her stomach with a wild kind of hunger. Her eyes closed as a soft moan rose in her throat. How could he be thinking of children with her if there was no emotion in him? A man interested in a body would certainly be thinking of ways to prevent that from happening, wouldn't he? She almost groaned aloud. If only she knew more about men. But Thorn hated what he felt for her, and made no secret of it. As far as she was concerned, she was only the gold digger his brother wanted to marry, a heartless flirt, a woman with her eye to the main chance. She sighed bitterly. None of that was true, but he'd never know. Because in two days, she'd be out of his life for good, and only the memories would remain. At least, she told herself, she had those, as bittersweet as they were.

The next day at breakfast, Thorn reminded them about the engagement party, which was being held that night. The way he said it sent chills up Sabina's spine.

"It will be formal," he told Sabina, his blue eyes challenging.

"I have a gown," she replied. "I won't disgrace you." She didn't look straight at him. She hadn't been able to since their confrontation in the woods, and she'd avoided him every minute she could—a fact of which he seemed angrily aware.

"Of course you won't," Al replied, studying his brother. "You look smug. Any particular reason?"

"I'm holding some good cards," the older man replied with a narrow glance in Sabina's direction. "What are the two of you planning to do today?"

"We're going down to New Orleans to get me a new dinner jacket," Al said smoothly. "My old one is getting a bit tight."

"Don't stay there too long," Thorn cautioned.

"Wouldn't dream of it," Al promised him.

They did go into New Orleans, but while they were there, they held a council of war with Jessica.

"I'm scared," the redhead confessed as they lunched in a small outdoor cafe. "What if

Thorn sees through the act? We don't get married until the day after tomorrow!''

"He doesn't suspect anything," Sabina assured her, patting her hand. "Trust us. We'll handle it.''

"It's just that it's so risky, even now." Jessica bit her lip, her eyes worshipping Al. "I'm afraid of Thorn.''

"He does inspire those feelings," Al said with a chuckle. "But not for much longer. Once we're actually married, there isn't a thing he can do.''

"And I'm taking good care of your ring," Sabina told her, grinning as she held it out. "How fortunate that we wear the same size!''

"There's no one I'd trust with it more," Jessica said warmly. "I feel that we're imposing on you, though. You're the one taking all the risks. And all the contempt. I can imagine what Thorn's put you through.''

"He hasn't bothered her," Al said with blessed ignorance.

But Jessica, watching the expressions that crossed her friend's face, wasn't fooled. A minute later, when Al went to the men's room, Jessica urgently leaned forward.

"Don't let Thorn hurt you," she pleaded. "Not even for our sakes. I don't want you to suffer."

Sabina searched her friend's eyes. "Jess, I'm in love with him."

Jess's eyes widened. "In love?"

"What do I do now?" Sabina whispered miserably. "It's the first time, and it hurts. And he thinks I'm nothing but a gold digger." She hid her face in her hands. "Oh, Jess, if he found out the truth about me, he wouldn't even soil his feet by walking on me."

"Stop talking like that," Jessica said with genuine concern. "You're every bit as good as he is."

"No," Sabina said. "Not in his mind. For all my small bit of fame, if he knew my background he wouldn't let me through the front door, and you know it."

"Oh, Sabina, what can I say? I feel so guilty!" Jessica said, frowning.

"I'll get over it," Sabina said. "All I have to do is live through the next couple of days. I'll grit my teeth. And then I'll be on the road. Maybe then, when I'm away from him, it won't bother me so much."

"And Thorn?" Jessica said probingly. "How does he feel?"

"He wants me."

Jessica sighed. "Oh, I see."

"Here's Al back. Don't give me away, please. I couldn't bear to have him know how I feel about his brother," Sabina pleaded. "Thorn would chew me up like candy if he knew!"

"I won't say a word." Jessica smiled as Al came back. "Hi, pal," she said, leaning over to give him a peck on the cheek.

"Hi, yourself," he said lovingly.

Watching them, Sabina felt like crying. If only Thorn could look at her that way, talk to her that way, just once. But that was a pipe dream. She'd learned to her sorrow that reality was painful. Thorn would never be hers. The most she could hope for was that she might linger in his memory as the one woman who got away.

That night, the house was filled with guests enjoying a catered buffet supper and dancing to a live band. It was the Saturday night before Easter Sunday, and Sabina thought she'd never seen such elegant clothes before. Her own strappy gown looked simple by comparison, which was probably what Thorn had intended. She might buy one expensive used dress, but her budget didn't allow her to buy several. This was the one she'd worn to Al's party, and she wondered if Thorn recognized it. He gave her a mock toast from across the room, and she turned away, hurt.

"He did that deliberately, didn't he?" Jessica asked. They'd escaped for a minute alone in the ladies' room.

"Baiting me," Sabina said with a sigh. "You can't imagine what it's been like. If I didn't like you so much..."

"I love you," Jessica said fervently, and hugged her. "Someday, somehow, I'll make it up to you."

"Are you happy, my friend?" Sabina asked with a tiny smile.

In her black satin dress, with her flaming red hair cascading over her shoulders, Jess was a vision. "Deliriously. I only hope it happens for you, too, one of these days."

"It would be a pity if it did," she replied carelessly. "I don't want marriage, and an affair is out of the question."

"But, Sabina, one day you'll want a family."

She winced. "No."

"With the right man, it would be different," Jessica assured her. "Your children would be wanted, loved."

Sabina's soft gray eyes widened as she thought about having a little boy with dark, waving hair and ice-blue eyes. Her heart skipped wildly. It was pure unadulterated stupidity. She had to stop thinking about Thorn that way.

"Are you all right? You're very pale," Jessica said softly.

"All right?" She was remembering the way it felt to kiss Thorn, and she burned all over. "Yes. I'm all right. Let's go back."

Al came up to them, fighting the urge to stare at Jessica. "Well, let's see if we can throw the wolf off the track, shall we?" he asked Sabina. "Jess, I wish there was some other way."

"We could leave the country," Jess murmured. "There wouldn't be an easier way, with Thorn."

"Miss Cane?"

Thorn's deep, slow voice rang out and all at once Sabina noticed that the crowd had stopped dancing and everyone was looking at her. She felt like a criminal being fingered, not like an up and coming celebrity in the entertainment world. But despite her modest dress, she held her head high and moved toward him gracefully. His eyes followed her movements with a tangible hunger and something oddly like pride.

"I've told our guests that you have quite a talent with music. How about doing something for us?"

"I'd be delighted," she said, approaching the small combo, which boasted two guitarists, a drummer and a pianist. They were much younger than The Bricks and Sand Band, but the pianist had style. She went straight toward him.

Thorn was expecting some raucous tune, so that he could embarrass her in front of his elegant guests. But the joke was going to be on him. She smiled secretively as she told the pianist what she wanted. And, fortunately, his training enabled him to provide the accompaniment she needed. Otherwise, she'd have had to sing a capella.

She turned to face the group. "I don't think I have to introduce this piece," she said with a faint smile in Thorn's direction. "I'm sure most of you will recognize it immediately." She nodded toward the pianist.

Thorn settled back against the door with a brandy snifter in his lean hand, his face mocking, challenging. *Conceited little girl,* he was saying without words, *you expect these very elite people to know your pitiful rock songs?*

She nodded toward Thorn then smiled at Jess and Al, who were almost jumping up and down with glee.

The pianist began, and she drew in a deep breath and suddenly burst into the exquisite aria from Puccini's "Madama Butterfly." The crowd stood completely still in the large room, as if every breath was suddenly held. Eyes widened as the piercingly clear voice rang out, as the sweep and flow and dramatic intensity of her voice told the well-known story in classic operatic style. When the melody broke into the high, achingly sweet notes near the end, tears were rolling down the cheeks of two of the women listening. And as she held the final note there was a shattering as if of glass. She finished. As she was bowing, she looked toward the back of the room, where Thorn had been standing. Only a tiny pile of broken crystal attested to the fact that he'd even been there at all.

"*Bravo!*" came the cries from the guests. "*Bravo, bravo!*"

"My dear," one tall matron said as she rushed toward Sabina, "I understood Thorn to say that you were a rock singer!"

"Yes," Sabina said with a smile. "You see, I couldn't afford to go to New York to study. It was my dream, but I'm finding a niche for myself in pop music. At least I can still sing the arias."

"And beautifully," the matron said, tears still in her eyes. "So beautifully. It was a privilege to listen to you."

"Thank you." With a final smile for the older woman, Sabina rejoined Al and Jessica as the band started up again.

"He broke the glass," Al said quietly, nodding toward the crystal on the floor.

"Did he hurt himself?" Sabina asked, concerned.

"I don't know."

Without thinking she rushed out the door and down the hall toward his study. The door was ajar. She pushed it open and walked in, her eyes searching for Thorn. He was at the window, smoking a cigarette.

"Thorn?"

He turned, his eyes dark and threatening, his face hard.

"Your hand…"

"Hand?" He lifted the free one and stared at it. He seemed not to have noticed that it was cut.

"I'll dress it for you," she said quietly. She went ahead into the half bath beyond the desk and riffled through the cabinet for antiseptic and a bandage.

He joined her, filling the small room, glaring down at her. His presence overwhelmed her, but she didn't speak. She bathed his hand, loving the calloused feel of it, the dark beauty of its leanness, its flat nails. She washed away the smear of blood and checked the cut for slivers of glass.

"I've never heard anything so beautiful," he said absently. "Your voice is a gift."

She laughed. "Yes, I suppose it is. I wanted a career in opera, you see. But I never had that kind of money. Training is expensive. I scrimped and saved to get what I could, but... circumstances made it impossible for me to continue."

"I knew you were penniless. I didn't know about the operatic aspirations, though," he said blankly.

"Don't try to cut me up, please," she said quietly. "I'm not nearly the threat you seem to think I am." She looked up as she put the bandage in place. "My life hasn't been easy. Don't make it any harder for me."

He reached out and gently touched her cheek, and his eyes narrowed. "Then get out, while you can. I've got a trump card. Don't make me play it in front of Al."

She smiled gently. "Trump card? You make me sound like a public enemy."

"You are," he said under his breath. His jaw tautened. "You're the most dangerous woman I've ever known."

She sighed as she put away the bandages and antiseptic. "Well, I'm glad to know that."

"Give Al back the ring, now, and we'll call it quits."

"Why?" she asked, her eyes searching his.

"Because you'll be cheating him. And me." He tossed the cigarette into the sink, where it hissed going out in the residue of water. "Sabina, we can't live under the same roof without sleeping together. Al's my brother. I love him. But I want you. And, God help me, wanting you is a fever I can't put out. One day, one night, it will be the way it was in the woods," he said huskily, watching her blush. "Except that I won't be able to stop in time. You know that, damn you!"

She searched his eyes. "You really care about Al, don't you?" she asked.

"Yes, I care," he said harshly. His eyes were devouring her face. He started to touch her and then drew back. "Sometimes I almost forget what kind of woman you really are, for all that soft innocence that drives me mad." He drew in a sharp breath and turned away from her. "Forget it. I must be going soft in my old age. Let's rejoin the rest. I'll even announce the engagement for you."

He strode ahead of her with his face set in rigid lines, his long legs making short work of the hall. Cutting straight through the crowd, he poured himself a glass of whiskey. When he turned, with a reckless, do-it-or-die look on his face, Sabina knew immediately that the war wasn't over. It was just beginning.

"Ladies and gentlemen, I'd like to make an announcement," he said, lifting his glass to get everyone's attention. "My brother, Al, has chosen a fiancée. May I introduce to you his choice. Miss Sabina Cane," he said, toasting her, his smile deliberately cruel as he concluded, "Sabina Cane, the illegitimate daughter of a New Orleans lady of the evening and one of her many paying admirers."

Sabina felt the blood drain from her face, but she didn't falter. She merely stared straight into Thorn's eyes. She didn't glance over her shoulder, where Al's expression was murderous, or to her side, where Jessica's face was contorted with pity.

The crowd split, clearing a path for her as she walked toward Thorn. She didn't miss a step. Her face was white, her eyes dark with pain and hurt, but she faced him bravely.

She didn't know where the courage was coming from, because inside part of her had died. All the long years she'd kept her secret, held it back, forbidden Jessica even to mention it aloud. And here the oil baron was, producing it like an incubus, taunting her with it in front of his elegant guests.

"Congratulations," she said unsteadily. "You've found me out. But let me tell you all of it, oil baron. My mother was in love with a boy who went away to Vietnam and didn't come back. He left her pregnant and her family threw her out into the streets. She wasn't eligible for welfare because she made a few dollars too much in tips from a waitressing job. Her earnings were just enough to pay the rent, but not much more. When I was born, she took on a night job as well, to support us. But after a few years of that, her health gave out." She straightened, aware of the hush around them, aware of the frozen expression on Thorn's dark face.

"The one thing she had in abundance was beauty. So when she couldn't get any other kind of job, she accepted a date with a wealthy merchant. He was the first. He bought my first pair of shoes, and other trinkets,'' she added, watching the word register in his narrow eyes. ''The second was a shipping tycoon, a friend of the merchant. He paid off the overdue rent and bought us a whole week's worth of groceries as well. We'd been getting scraps from the butcher to make soup until then, because we didn't have enough money for anything more.'' Thorn's face was so drawn by now that it looked pasty. ''There were other men after that. She'd discovered the luxury of having enough to eat and warm clothes and necessities for her little girl. Then she met Harry. Harry was rich, but he had this one little idiosyncrasy. He liked to beat her until she couldn't stand up....'' Her voice was beginning to tremble now, as it all came back. She swallowed and straightened again. ''She loved him desperately, and when he was sober, he seemed to love her, too. But one night, he had too much to drink. And he beat her to death. Right in front of me.''

''Oh, God,'' Thorn whispered, his voice tormented, his eyes wild.

She drew in a slow breath. "So I was sent to the local orphanage, where I learned how to work for a living. I've been doing it ever since. And trying to live down the past. Ironically, until tonight, there was only one other person in the whole world who knew it. Now," she turned to the guests, who were staring helplessly at her, "I suppose I'll be dragging it behind me like a chain as long as I live. There's just one other little thing. This is what you wanted, I believe, Hamilton Regan Thorndon the Third."

And she tugged off her ring and turned to hand it to Al.

"Just a minute," Al said, coming forward. He faced his taller, older brother with venom in his eyes. "That was unwarranted, and unworthy of you. And if you don't apologize, I'll knock you down, big brother."

Thorn gave him a considering look and nodded. "Yes, it was unworthy," he said in a subdued tone. "And damned cruel. Miss Cane, I apologize for my lack of manners," he added, looking straight at Sabina.

Her eyes were so clouded with unshed tears, she was unable to see the lancing pain in his icy blue eyes. She only nodded, turned and left the room.

Thorn hadn't apologized for his insolence, only for his lack of manners, she thought hysterically. She packed quickly, dragging clothes from drawers and stuffing them into her carryall. She felt poleaxed. Devastated. Apparently, he'd done some checking into her past and come up with this—what had he called it— his trump card.

She laughed through tears as she finished packing. It was so cruel to throw that in her face, in front of all those people. So cruel!

The door opened and he was standing there. His eyes were dark, his face unsmiling, his posture stiff and strange.

"Did you bring a knife?" she asked. "I can only assume you intend to finish me off in private."

"I shouldn't have done that to you," he said in a tone she'd never heard him use. He had one hand deep in his pocket, the other holding a cigarette. "It was like tearing the wings from a butterfly, and about as satisfying. I had no right."

"Why bother about rights?" she asked,

smiling bitterly. "Nobody else ever did. I wasn't even a person when I was little. I was that love child down the street, Bessie's yard child. At the orphanage it was a little better. At least I didn't have to watch her with men." Her eyes clouded at the memory and Thorn actually flinched. "I knew she was doing it for me—I even understood—but that didn't make it any easier." She ground her teeth in an agony of rememance. "I hated her for a long time. Until he killed her." Her eyes closed and she shuddered, trying to blot out the memory. "It took years to get over that, and I was so alone. I missed her then," she whispered. "But I hated what she had to become, and I hated rich men dangling expensive gifts to lure her in, to tempt her. If her health had held out, maybe it would have been different. But she had to support us, and that was the only way she could find. Still I'll hate what she became until the day I die, and I'll hate rich men who made her that way. I won't be like her, I won't, I won't!"

She was crying openly, and Thorn's face had gone white. Absolutely white.

Her lower lip trembled and she fought for control. "This isn't much, is it?" She nodded toward the dress. "You wanted to show me up in front of your wealthy guests down there, and you did it, too. I don't have money to throw away on designer gowns. The clothes I wear are all secondhand, but I need to have them to perform in. Al says I'm the best bargain hunter around."

His eyes were fierce and the cigarette had to be burning his fingers, but he didn't even seem aware of it. He looked tormented. "I gave you that check…"

"I gave it to Al," she said wearily. "He's building a new wing for the hospital, a wing for disadvantaged children. The project we wanted your support for was a benefit to help build it. I endorsed the check and signed it over to him, to be donated in your name."

She turned away from his white face, which was drained of emotion, and life, and picked up her carryall. "As for the engagement, you'll find out soon enough that it was a sham, and why. Now go away, Mr. Thorndon the Third. Get out of my sight, before I get sick."

He stared at her, trying to find words. "I'll drive you home."

"No, you won't," she said sharply. "After

what you did to me downstairs, you won't drive me anyplace. I'll walk."

"Sabina," he whispered in anguish.

"Congratulations, you won," she said, her hot eyes glaring at him. "Aren't you proud of yourself, oil baron?"

"No," he growled. "I'm ashamed." His eyes searched her face one last time before he turned and went out the door, closing it gently behind him. Sabina glanced around the room slowly and went out behind him.

She met Al and Jessica as she started down the staircase.

"We'll drive you home," Al insisted. "I'm sorry. God, I'm so sorry!"

"Regrets don't accomplish anything, dear friend," she said with a wan smile. "Just get me out of here, please."

"I'll stay with you tonight," Jessica said firmly. "And no arguments. I won't leave you alone. Al, he may be your brother, but he's a monster."

"He's going to be a lonely one from now on," Al promised her. "We're getting married. All out in the open. And I'm forming my own company. We'll talk tomorrow. Thorn's really fixed things tonight.''

Sabina didn't say a word. She was in love with Thorn, and he'd shown her graphically that he didn't give a damn about her. She wondered if the pain would ever stop. She felt eyes watching as she went out the door, but she didn't turn. She couldn't have borne the sight of him. She still cared. Damn him, she still loved him.

Chapter Seven

Jessica's pale eyes narrowed with concern as Sabina sat huddled in her gown and robe drinking the coffee they'd brewed.

"Are you going to be all right?" Jess asked, breaking Sabina's trance.

"Of course I am," Sabina said coldly.

Jess saw right through the mask behind the stiff lip and the determined rigidity. "You really love that man, don't you?"

Sabina took a slow breath and a sip of the hot black coffee. "He doesn't deserve to be loved."

"I'm tempted to agree," Jessica said, watching the taller girl. "But I got a look at his face as we were going out the door. If I were old Juan, I'd hide all the guns tonight.''

''Did he look as if he might follow me home and shoot me as well?'' Sabina laughed hollowly, but there was curiosity in the question, too. She looked up, searching Jessica's face. ''Did he?''

''He looked as if he might blow his own brains out, if you want to know,'' she replied quietly. She wondered if she ought to tell her anguished friend the rest as well, that there had been a kind of loving anguish in Thorn's blue eyes.

''He'll get over it,'' Sabina said, leaning back in her chair wearily. ''When he's had time to reason it out, he'll decide that it was all my fault and he'll pat himself on the back for his brilliance. He saved Al from me, you know.''

''Al told him the truth.'' Jessica bit her lip. She hadn't meant to let that slip.

Sabina's face went stark white, her eyes as big as saucers. ''And what did Thorn say?''

Jess shifted restlessly. ''He didn't say anything, but Al had to call his dentist. Thorn knocked two teeth out.''

"Then what?" Sabina asked.

"Thorn stormed off to his study and locked the door." Jessica sighed. "Al figured he deserved the punch, and I think I deserve one, too, for what we've done to you and Thorn with this stupid deception," she added tearfully. "If we'd had any idea…"

"Thorn and I live in different worlds," Sabina said quietly. "You mustn't blame yourselves. It would never have amounted to anything. I would have been just another notch on his belt."

Jessica shook her head. "I'm afraid not. If it had only been that, Sabina, he wouldn't have minded hurting you. Al said he was like a wounded bear. Even the ranch foreman wouldn't go near him. He went to Al, and that was a first."

"All those people," Sabina said under her breath, closing her eyes. "All those exclusive people, knowing everything about me." She shuddered. "I don't know how I stood there and said those things to him."

"I was so proud of you," Jessica said. "So proud! You were every inch a lady, and it was Thorn who was getting the killing glances, darling, not you. No one's ever beaten him before."

Perhaps she'd beaten him, but at what cost? "Everyone will know now," she said dully. "We'll never get another job. I'll have to leave the band—"

"Stop that!" Jessica said firmly. "I won't let you feel sorry for yourself. You're just not the type."

"I could turn into the type right now." Sabina laughed bitterly.

"Can I fix you something to eat?"

"I'd like Thorn's heart, fried," she said with pure malice.

"Yes, I imagine so. How about some steamed liver, instead?"

Sabina laughed in spite of herself. "No. I don't want anything." She huddled closer in her robe. "Al was terrific, wasn't he?"

"Absolutely." Jessica's eyes warmed. "That was the first time he's ever stood up to Thorn, you know. I don't think it will be the last, despite the loss of his teeth. He didn't duck. He said he figured Thorn had the right."

Sabina hardly heard her. Her mind was drifting in and out of the past, shivering with the force of the memories. For years she'd fought to suppress them. Now they wouldn't be suppressed anymore.

The phone rang and Sabina stiffened.

Jessica soothed her. "It's probably Al." She got up and answered it. "Hello?" Her face went rigid, and she started to speak, but whoever was on the other end apparently said something that got her attention. She paused, glancing warily at Sabina. "Yes. Yes, I think so." She bit her lip. "I don't know if she'll listen, but I'll tell her. Yes. Yes. Good night."

She put down the receiver and turned. "Thorn," she said quietly.

Sabina's eyes grew as hard as diamonds. She averted her face.

"He wanted to make sure you had someone with you tonight," Jessica said, feeling the way. "He..." She hesitated. "He sounded odd."

"I don't care," Sabina said brutally. "I'll never care again. Let's get some sleep."

Jessica watched her friend walk out of the room. Sabina was too hurt right now to listen, but if his voice was any indication, Thorn was hurting, too. That concern had been real. Perhaps he hadn't quite realized it himself yet, but he'd destroyed the one thing of value in his life. Sabina had gotten closer to him than anyone else, and he'd lashed out at her with a fury. Al had said that. But the cruelty had backfired. It had cost him dearly. Jessica felt like a traitor to admit it, but she felt sorry for her future brother-in-law. Sabina and Thorn were so alike, both trapped in shells of their own making, keeping the world at bay so that it couldn't hurt them. She shook her head sadly and went to bed. Long after she had lain down, she heard Sabina's sobs.

Al and Jessica were married early Monday morning. It turned out to be more of an ordeal than Sabina had expected. She'd thought that, under the circumstances, Al would get one of his employees to stand up with him, but when she got to the small church, Thorn was there.

Sabina, in a neat beige suit, hesitated at the back pew. Jessica, in an oyster-colored street-length dress, came to meet her.

"He won't bother you," Jessica said gently. "Al made him promise."

Tears threatened to overflow Sabina's eyes.

She was still vulnerable, afraid of what he could do to her right now. She hesitated. "I almost didn't come," she confessed softly. "I... Dennis, our road manager, got an offer this morning for a gig at a fabulously well-known club in New York City. Right out of the blue, at a fantastic salary. We jumped at it, of course. We needed the job really bad, and I'm...not known in New York." She choked on the words.

"Nobody will know!" Jessica said firmly. "For heaven's sake, those people aren't going to run to the nearest newspaper and have it all dragged out on the front page! Even Thorn wouldn't do that to you!"

"Wouldn't he?" Sabina asked unsteadily. She stared at his back in the dark business suit he was wearing, at the dark hair that her fingers had stroked. So they'd dulled his fangs, had they? She still felt savaged, and her pride was in tatters. The humiliation he'd heaped on her was fresh enough to burn. She'd stood up to him before, and she wasn't going to run. But her heart pounded wildly with every step she took with Jessica to the front of the small

church, where the minister, Al and Thorn
waited.

Thorn turned as she came down the aisle.
He watched her with an intensity that almost
tripped her up. His face was pale and drawn.
There were deep, harsh shadows under his
haunted blue eyes. So you can't sleep either,
she thought coldly. Good! I'm glad you can't
sleep!

She edged around him without actually
meeting his searching gaze and stood on the
other side of Jessica for the brief ceremony. All
through it, as the minister spoke the age-old
words, she felt her heart aching for what she
might have had with Thorn in another time,
another place. Tears blurred her vision of the
minister and she bit her lip to keep the tears at
bay. As he spoke the words "with my body, I
thee worship," her eyes went helplessly, involuntarily to Thorn, and found him staring at
her. She quickly dropped her gaze to the car-
peted floor.

Thorn, she whispered silently. Thorn! How
much he must have hated her, to be so cruel.
His conscience was bothering him. He was
guilt-ridden, but she had to remember that it

was only that. He'd never cared. He'd only wanted her. And now he pitied her. Her eyes closed. That hurt the most, that all he felt was pity. She'd rather have his contempt.

It was all over in minutes. Al kissed Jessica with gusto, and then turned to be congratulated by the minister and Thorn. Sabina brushed Jessica's flushed cheek with cool lips and grinned at her.

"Be happy," she said softly.

"We'll see you soon, when we're back from Nassau."

"Not unless you don't go at all," Sabina said with a forced laugh, aware of Thorn's deep, slow voice behind her. "The band and I have to leave for New York tonight. We'll be at the club for two weeks, and Dennis said something about a video we may film there. Some agent heard us in Savannah and thinks we may have video appeal, how about that?"

"Things are looking up." Jessica grinned. "I'm so glad for you."

Sabina nodded. "Yes, I'm looking forward to it."

Jessica stared at her uneasily. Sabina was as pale as Thorn, and she seemed subdued, haunted. Of course, Thorn's presence here was enough to do that to her.

"I thought you still had a week to go at the club here," Jessica said under her breath.

Sabina shifted from one foot to the other. "Al let us out of it, with no argument from the other partner," she said, refusing even to say Thorn's name.

"Where can I write to you?" Jessica asked.

"Send it to the apartment house, in care of Mr. Rafferty," Sabina said, her voice dull and lackluster. "He said he'd hold my mail for me until I got back. I packed this morning."

The two women embraced warmly and Sabina turned to kiss Al, gently and with genuine affection. "Congratulations, pal," she said with a hint of her old brightness. "Take good care of my best friend, will you?"

"You bet," Al said. He looked radiant, but his green eyes were narrow with concern. "Take care of yourself, you hear?"

"Of course."

He kissed her cheek. "Thanks. I'm only beginning to realize just how much Jess and I really owe you for today," he added quietly.

"Just be happy. See you," she said with a

forced grin. She turned, trying to get past Thorn without speaking, but he wouldn't move. Al and Jessica discreetly moved off with the minister, deserting her. She clutched her purse convulsively and stared at his striped tie.

"Well?" she asked tightly.

His quiet, darkened eyes studied her, memorized her. His hands slid into his pockets. "I'd like an hour with you."

"I don't have an hour. I don't have five seconds for you, oil baron," she said curtly.

"I expected that you'd react that way. Maybe I can condense it. I didn't know the truth. Does that count for anything?"

She finally lifted her eyes and had to fight not to throw herself into his arms. He looked and sounded genuinely sorry. But if she'd hoped for more than a surface regret, it wasn't there. Or he was hiding it well.

"Should it?" she asked. "You savaged me!" Her lower lip trembled, and he looked violent for an instant. "I never told anyone about my past, not a soul, except Jessica!"

His face hardened. "Didn't anyone ever tell you it's dangerous to keep secrets? I tried to make you give the ring back without going that far, but you wouldn't do it.''

''I couldn't,'' she returned hotly. ''I'd promised to divert you until they could get married.''

He ran a rough hand through his dark hair. ''Al could have leveled with me at the outset! I like Jessica, I always have. I wouldn't have fought him if I'd known he was that much in love with her.''

''He was afraid of you,'' she said, her voice short. ''He said you'd put an end to it. They're the only friends I've ever had, so I agreed to help them. I wanted to pay you back for the way you'd treated me....'' She had to stop as the rage threatened to choke her. She could barely see the shadow that darkened his eyes. ''And you...trying to buy me for the night—'' She laughed shakily. ''My whole childhood was one long procession of men with money. You can't imagine how I hate rich men and desperate women who let themselves be bought!''

''Maybe I understand better than you think,'' he said. ''We talked occasionally. You might have told me. It would have saved a lot of grief.''

"And give you the perfect weapon to use against me?" she burst out. "Wouldn't you have loved that! An illegitimate orphan with a tramp for a mother, from the back streets of New Orleans."

"Stop it," he said roughly. "I never would have hurt you—"

"What would you call stripping my soul naked in front of Beaumont's finest?"

He looked around the church uncomfortably. "I've apologized," he said tersely.

"Some apology," she returned. "I told Jessica that you'd find some way to put the onus on me. You don't make mistakes, do you, oil baron?"

His eyes darkened as they looked down into hers, and his jaw clenched. His chest rose and fell heavily with each breath. "You don't know me."

"Oh, yes, I do," she said fervently. "I know you inside out. You're so warm and safe in that shell you wear that you'll never let anyone else in it with you. You'll keep the whole world away, and tell yourself you're satisfied. You'll grow old, with no one to love or be loved by. You'll have that fortune you've made, and you'll have all the women you can buy. But you'll be alone until you die.''

His breathing was audible now, his eyes cutting. ''Are you through?'' he asked.

''Almost.'' She searched his face, feeling her will cave in, her body tremble with remembered pleasure, with the bittersweet agony of loving him. ''I came too close, didn't I?'' she asked quietly. ''You didn't just attack me to save Al. You hated me because I saw too much. I saw beneath that mask you wear.''

His eyes flashed anger, his tall body tensed. ''Get out of my life,'' he said in a harsh whisper.

''I thought I'd already done that,'' she said lifting her chin. ''You win. You always win. You even told me so. I should have listened. Goodbye, Hamilton Regan Thorndon the Third,'' she said with a forced, broken laugh. ''I hope you and your money will be very happy together.''

''If you're going, go!'' he said icily.

She knew she'd never forget that hard face, not as long as she lived. She turned away, turning her eyes down. Her steps quickened as she started back down the aisle.

"Al...Jessica...see you!" she called. And Thorn watched her every step as she ran blindly from the church.

The next few weeks seemed to pass like slow motion. Sabina wasn't even aware of being tired, of pushing herself as she and the band gave one performance after another. But she did, exhausting her body and soul, as if to purge herself of the painful memories.

They filmed the video their first week in New York. It was exciting, and Sabina's head reeled when she heard about the thousands of dollars it had cost. All Dennis told her was that they had a backer, but he kept changing the subject when she asked who. Not that it mattered, she supposed. It was the newest way to break into the recording field, anyway. One video on the music channel could make or break a new group, and she was almost sure that theirs was going to be a sensation.

The young production crew that filmed it for them was wildly supportive, impressed with the quality of Sabina's voice and the throbbing rhythm and harmony of the song Ricky had written. It was titled "Ashes and Wind," and they decided on a rooftop fantasy, with Sabina wearing black tattered chiffon and being chased across rooftops with smoking chimneys by a man in a top hat carrying a white cane. It was funky and wild, and a lot of fun.

Ricky Turner was overwhelmed with the finished product. It was in the can days later, and in a month it would be released on the cable music channel.

The group was getting advance publicity, too, with ads on television and radio and in the print media, and their opening at the New York club netted them some flattering reviews. The advertising would surely boost sales of "Ashes and Wind," Ricky told them smugly. And if Sabina hadn't been so involved in performing and trying to get over Thorn all at once, she might have wondered about the amount of money all this was costing. And where it was coming from.

"The advertising is drawing big crowds," Dennis mentioned one afternoon, excited about the fact that the club had already booked them for two additional weeks. "And next week, the video will be out. We're going great, people. Just great.''

"Yes, we sure are,'' Ricky murmured. ''I just hope nothing goes wrong.''

"Worrywart,'' Sabina said accusingly. ''You just sit and brood on things to worry about, and nothing ever goes wrong.''

''That's what worries me.''

She threw up her hands and walked away.

The New York club was an exclusive one, over fifty floors up near Rockefeller Center, and the city spread out below in a jeweled fantasy at night. Couples held hands at their tables while the band performed the soft rock music it was growing famous for, and Sabina felt a twinge of envy. It had never bothered her before. But then, she'd never known what love was until Thorn walked into her life.

The memory of him made her sad, bruised her heart. It had been a tragic thing all the way around. If she'd had good sense, she'd never have agreed to run interference for Al. But then, he and Jessica wouldn't be married now and looking forward to any kind of life together.

Her eyes misted over as she thought what it

might have been like if she and Hamilton Regan Thorndon the Third had met under normal circumstances. If, that first night at Al's party, they'd been strangers altogether and could have started from scratch.

But just as quickly, she remembered his harsh accusation that last night, about her illegitimacy, her mother, and she went hot all over with rage. She wasn't good enough for him. Eventually, he'd have found it out even if they'd started dating and Al hadn't been in the picture. He'd have found out about her past, and he'd have walked away. When Hamilton Thorndon married, it would be a society ingenue, a Houston oil heiress or a New Orleans society woman. It certainly wouldn't be an illegitimate child and orphan.

As long as she lived, she'd remember his face at the church. If only it had been something deeper than a guilty conscience, she might have been tempted to throw herself into his powerful arms and take up residence. But, of course, it hadn't been anything deeper. Because he wasn't capable of it. Especially with a woman like her.

Bitterness replaced her frustration and she

pushed harder, rehearsed longer, put her whole heart into her performances. She'd show him. Her past wasn't going to hold her back. She'd make a name for herself, have the whole world at her feet. And then he'd see what he'd passed up; he'd be sorry.

She looked at herself in the mirror, sighing. Sure. Look what Thorn passed up, she thought miserably, seeing dark eyes dominating a white, drawn face. Even her hair was lackluster, and she was losing weight rapidly. She turned away from her reflection, demoralized.

When she got back to the club, Ricky was glaring as the technicians finished the set and adjusted the heavy lighting.

"I don't like the way that light's hanging," he muttered, pointing to one of the small, low-hanging spotlights.

"You're just overanxious, as usual," she said accusingly. "Come and have some coffee with me. I want to ask you about that new number we did in the video."

He shrugged philosophically as she dragged him away. "Okay," he said. "Maybe it won't come crashing down on your pretty head."

"If it does, I'll remember that I told you to leave it alone," she promised.

The words were prophetic. That night, as they started into their routine, the small spotlight swiveled and came loose. It crashed down onto the stage to the hysterical screams of the packed audience, hitting the side of Sabina's head.

She was knocked out as the hardware still attached to it cut into her shoulder. It wasn't a big light, fortunately, but it was heavy enough to do some damage.

Sabina regained consciousness in the hospital, her eyes unfocusing, her body hurting. The last thing she'd remembered was singing a song and hearing a yell from the door of the club, a tormented yell in a voice she'd thought she recognized. But then the spotlight made impact. She'd thrown up an arm and felt shattering pain in her head and shoulder. And then, darkness.

"Come on, come on," came a harsh, commanding voice. Her hand was being restrained, gripped in something rough and warm that wouldn't let go. "You're tough, tulip. You even beat me. Now come on and fight your way back. I'm not letting go until you do. Come on!''

Her eyes blinked. It had been warm and comfortable in her oblivion and now she was hurting like hell. She moaned.

''That's it,'' the voice continued, softer now, coaxing. ''That's better. Open your eyes, honey, let me see your eyes.''

Weren't they open already? How odd they felt. She struggled and her heavy eyelids slowly lifted. There was someone bending over her. She blinked and her eyes opened a little wider. A man. An older man, with a stethoscope. She glanced around numbly and saw the maze of machines connected to her body, in a tiny room whose window faced a nursing desk. She tried to move, but there were wires everywhere. She blinked again.

''Miss Cane, do you feel any discomfort?'' the elderly man asked.

She had to lick her dry lips before she could answer. ''Hurts,'' she managed. ''Head. And…my…my shoulder.'' She tried to move, but the pain was too great. She was gently pressed back into the pillows.

''You've been in a coma, but you're going

to be all right now. We're going to give you something for the pain," he said. "You'll be fine."

Her eyes closed again. It was too much of an effort to keep them open.

The next time she opened them, it was to find herself in a hospital room. Her mind still felt foggy, but the pain had lessened considerably. She glanced toward her right shoulder and found it bandaged. It felt odd when she moved, stiff and sore. There was something tugging uncomfortably at her temple, too. She reached up slowly with her left hand and found something like thread there, and raw skin. Stitches!

"Hello."

That voice.... She frowned drowsily, turning her head. Even half unconscious and full of painkillers, she reacted to the sight of him. She lay there helpless, looking, staring, loving.

"Thorn," she whispered.

He leaned over her, his face looking tired, his blue eyes soft. Sabina couldn't believe her eyes. She had to be dreaming.

He was wearing a dark suit and he looked rumpled. The white shirt had blood on it. She frowned. Blood? Where had he gotten that? And it was a dinner jacket, not a suit. Her eyes went back up to his.

"Are you in pain, darling?" he asked softly.

She was delirious. He couldn't call her darling. Anyway, he wasn't there. She closed her eyes. "Sleepy," she mumbled, and it was the last thing she remembered.

Daylight streamed in through the blinds, disturbing her sleep. She brushed at it, as if it were a fly she could shoo away.

"No," she muttered. "Go away. Too bright...."

"I'll close the blinds."

Had somebody spoken? She heard a chair creak and hard, heavy footsteps. She turned her head on the cool pillow and saw him again. The pain had returned so this time she knew she wasn't dreaming. It really was Thorn.

Chapter Eight

Sabina stared at him with eyes that wouldn't quite focus. Painkillers and weariness had made them foggy.

"How do you feel?" he repeated, his voice deeply textured and slow.

Her eyes searched his face blankly as she tried to fit the pieces together. He hated her. He wanted her out of his life. He'd shamed her and humiliated her and told her to go. Why was he here?

"Terrible," she said, her voice thin and weak. Restlessly, she turned her disheveled head against the soft white pillowcase. She felt numb discomfort. "That light...." She tried to get up.

"Settle down. You'll tear something loose," he said curtly. Firm but gentle hands nestled her back down into the pillows.

"My shoulder...." She tried to move it, but there were bandages. And the other arm had a Styrofoam pad under the forearm and a tube leading to a needle in the wrist. "What—"

"An IV," Thorn said. He sat down in the chair beside the bed and leaned back. "You've got a nasty concussion," he said quietly. "And a bruised shoulder, and some cuts and bruises. But your doctor says that if you keep improving, you'll be out of here within five days, and back at work in about a month."

She blinked. None of this was making sense. And why was he here? Her eyes went to his stained shirt. He was still wearing the dinner jacket, and the same shirt.

"You've got blood on your shirt," she faltered.

"So what?" he asked. His eyes were anything but soothing.

"How long have I been here?"

"Three days," he said, and there was a world of meaning in his tone.

"Were you…at the club when it happened?" she persisted.

He sighed roughly, grabbed an ashtray already half full of stubs, and lit another cigarette. "No," he said a moment later. "I was at a dinner party in Manhattan. I'd planned to stop by later. Dennis phoned me as soon as he'd called for an ambulance." He laughed shortly. "The ambulance and I got there at the same time. I rode in with you."

She didn't understand any of it. "Why are you here?" she asked, confused. "You hate me."

His angry glare seemed to underline her statement. "Who else have you got?" he asked bluntly. "Al's in Saudi Arabia, with Jessica, on a business trip for me. Dennis and Ricky and the guys were willing to stay with you, of course, but they had to finish off the club engagement with another vocalist."

"Another singer? Who?" she asked, her ears perking up.

"Does it matter?"

She sighed, feeling uncomfortable and confused and thoroughly miserable. Her big chance and someone else was taking her place, while Thorn sat there glaring at her as if he despised her. Her eyes closed. Tears welled up and spilled out.

"Oh, for God's sake, not that!" Thorn growled.

Her lower lip trembled, too, and she bit it to keep it still. "I'm being taken care of, obviously," she said, forcing her eyes open. "Thank you for all your concern, but why don't you go home? I can take care of myself now. I'm good at it. I've had years of practice."

He got up, looming over her, with one hand in his pocket and the other holding the cigarette. The blue eyes that glittered down at her were impossible to read.

"What do I have to go home to?" he asked bluntly.

That threw her. She dropped her gaze to the sheet. She wanted to tug it up and wipe her wet eyes, but both hands were immobilized. "You've got your women, oil baron." She laughed coldly.

"I'm alone," he said. His eyes studied her up and down and returned to her face, where a stark white bandage was taped around her temple and her neck. "I have no one."

Unable to meet his gaze, she stared blankly at the needle in the back of her hand. "Join the club."

He drew in a slow breath. "You're going to be out of commission for a while."

The implications were just beginning to get through to her. She looked up at him in a daze. Yes, she'd need looking after, and a place to rest. Since Jessica wasn't around now, what would she do?

"There's no need to panic," Thorn said, lifting the cigarette to his mouth. "You're coming home with me. I'll take care of you until you're back on your feet."

"Like hell you will!" she burst out, horrified at the thought of being completely at his mercy for weeks.

He lifted his shoulders and let them fall. "I expected that," he said absently, studying her. "But what else can we do, tulip? God knows, you can't be left alone."

"Get me back to New Orleans," she said. "I can stay in my own apartment. Mr. Rafferty will look after me."

His face hardened. He turned away. "Rafferty thinks you're a cross between a saint and the good fairy."

She stared at him nervously. "How do you know?"

His broad shoulders shifted as he stared out through the window blinds. "I wanted to see where you lived."

She shuddered. "Why?"

When he turned, his face was expressionless. "It's a hovel," he said coldly.

Her eyes blazed. "It is not! It's a decent, economical place to live, and I have good neighbors! They'll take care of me!"

He took a final draw from his cigarette and crushed it out angrily. "Mr. Rafferty is hardly able to take care of himself. How do you think he'd manage those stairs to your apartment several times a day?"

Tears threatened to come again, as she realized how right he was, how helpless she was.

"Yes, I know, you're proud and you hate being obligated to me in any way," he said quietly. "But you don't have much choice."

But being near him, living with him...how

would she bear it? Especially knowing how he felt about her, how he hated her.

"You said that I was afraid to let anyone come close to me. That I was afraid of involvement. Aren't you the same way?"

She felt trapped. "Yes, but…"

He reached down, drawing his fingers softly against her cheek, her mouth, holding her eyes with his. "I've hurt you more than I ever meant to, Sabina," he said gently. "For God's sake, let me make amends in the only way I can."

"To salve your conscience?" she asked unsteadily.

He stared at her mouth, running his lean finger sensuously around its perfect bow shape. "If that's what you want to believe."

"It was only desire. You said so."

"I did, didn't I?" he murmured.

"Thorn—"

"I'll take care of you."

"But, the band—" she moaned.

"They can live without you for a few weeks," he said. "Once that video hits the market next week, you'll be a legend in your own time, anyway."

That hardly registered. Between her foggy mind and his devastating nearness, she wasn't thinking straight. "How did you know about the video?"

He tilted her chin up a little more. "Never mind how I knew." His voice sounded oddly strained. "Listen, I need to go back to my hotel and change. Will you be all right now?"

She blinked, suddenly realizing that if she'd been here for three days, he had, too. She knew because he was wearing the same clothes he had on when she was brought in.

"You've been here all this time?" she burst out, aghast.

He brushed the unruly hair away from her pale face. "Yes."

"But why?"

"I like hospitals," he growled. "I love sitting in emergency rooms and watching people in green uniforms pass by, and sitting in waiting rooms in the intensive-care unit begging to see you for five damned minutes three times a day! And there's nothing quite as comfortable as a straight chair in a waiting room.

"You didn't have to—" she began.

"How could I leave you, for God's sake?"

he said, and his eyes wandered hungrily over her face. "You were in a coma when we got you here!"

"Coma?" she parroted.

"Until you opened your eyes and started grumbling at me early this morning, I wasn't sure you'd come out of it at all, despite what the doctor said."

"You can't pretend you cared whether I did or not," she said coldly.

"You can't imagine how I felt," he said in a rough undertone.

"That's right," she replied abruptly, giving him a burning look. "Remember me? The illegitimate kid from the wrong side of the—"

She suddenly stopped as a lean, hard finger settled over her mouth.

"Don't," he said, regret forming a mask of strain over his handsome face. "I tried to tell you at Al's wedding how deeply I regretted that. You might not believe it, but I hurt myself as much as I hurt you."

Her face turned into the pillow as it all came back, a bitterly vivid memory.

"I disgraced myself, you know," he said after a long pause, sounding ironic and self-mocking. Her eyes came up to meet his and he smiled. "That's right. None of the people who came to that dinner party will even speak to me now. And the matron who cried when you sang even went so far as to sell her stock in my company. How's that for revenge?"

She showed a hint of a smile. He seemed to be more amused than angered by the reaction. "You don't mind?"

"Of course I mind," he murmured. "I'm never invited to luncheons or formal dinners these days. I'm having to survive on old Juan's cooking, and he's mad at me, too. He burns everything he sets before me. Juan is another of your instant conquests," he added ruefully.

She flushed, lowering her eyes to his stained shirt. Odd where that stain was, just about where her bleeding head would have rested if he'd held her.

"If you'll come home with me," he said, "Juan will have to cook good meals, and I'll gain back some of the weight I've lost. So will you. You've lost a bit yourself."

"I've been working hard," she said.

"Yes. Dennis told me." He stuck both hands in his pockets. "Come on. I dare you."

Dare. The old word from her childhood brought her eyes up. She stared at him, taking in the mocking smile, the challenge in his blue eyes. "All right," she said. "I'll go with you."

He smiled slowly. "Think of it as a crash course in human relations. You can teach me to be human, and I'll teach you how to be a woman."

Her body tingled. "I don't want to become a..."

"Hush." He bent and kissed her mouth tenderly, barely touching her. "I won't seduce you, even if you beg. Okay?"

She could hardly catch her breath. "You could make me beg," she whispered with painful honesty.

"I know. Is that what frightens you?" he asked gently.

She nodded. Her eyes were so close to his that she could see their dark blue outline, the wrinkles beside his eyes.

After a pause, he said, "You aren't the only one who's vulnerable. I'd better let someone know you're awake." He said it as if the weakness irritated him. He pressed the call button and before she could get her mind together enough to question him, he was out the door and the nurse was inside making a condition check.

"How lucky you are," the young nurse said with a smile as she took Sabina's temperature. "The ICU staff bent the rules a little for Mr. Thorndon when they saw what his presence was doing for you. He sat and held your hand and talked to you all the time. You kept having seizures and he sat there like a man possessed, watching us work on you." She shook her head with a sigh. "We were all afraid you wouldn't come out of it. Comas are so unpredictable, and we're helpless to do anything about them in circumstances like these. We just have to sit and wait."

The thermometer came out and Sabina stared at the nurse. "Thorn stayed with me all that time?"

"He sure did." She sighed. "What a heavenly male. Lucky, lucky you." She grinned, finished her tasks, and breezed out again.

Thorn was back less than an hour later, still worn but a little more relaxed. He had an attaché case with him, and after sitting down in a chair beside the bed, he opened it and took out a sheaf of papers.

"Go to sleep," he told her. "I'll sit here and work."

From his pocket, he pulled out a pair of reading glasses, tinted ones that looked more like pilot's sunglasses. She smiled faintly at the way he looked in them as he bent over reams of paper. He was wearing a white turtleneck sweater with a blue blazer and dark blue slacks, highly polished boots and a cream-white Stetson. She looked at him with adoration.

He looked up, smiling warmly at her. "Go to sleep," he repeated gently.

"Aren't you tired?" she said drowsily. "You need some rest, too."

"I can't rest away from you," he said quietly.

If only she wasn't so sleepy. But her head had been throbbing and she'd asked for something to kill the pain. The injection of Demerol was just beginning to work.

"Don't... leave me," she whispered sleepily.

"Never again," came the soft reply, but she was past hearing.

* * *

A week from the day she'd entered the hospital, Thorn took her back to Texas. She was weak, and she'd suffered some vertigo and nausea those first days out of intensive care. But now she was on the way to recovery, and it felt wonderful to be outside again, even in the bitter cold.

Christmas was barely a week away. So was the band's new video. She smiled, remembering the brief visits the guys had made to her room, when they could get past Thorn. He was determined that she should rest, and ran interference like a professional. Ricky and Dennis managed a few minutes, long enough to tell her how well the club engagement was going, despite the fact that their stand-in vocalist was male. Anyway, they said, the video was going to be the big thing, and it would be on the music channel within days. She was to look for it. Thorn's ranch was beyond the limits of the cable company, but he had a satellite dish, so they'd be able to get it anyway.

She was surprised to find the ranch fully decorated for Christmas, all brightly lit and an enormous fir tree loaded with decorations, and a kitchen full of baked delights. Under the tree were dozens of presents. Sabina had a down-stairs room, so that she wouldn't have to risk climbing stairs.

"Is your mother coming for Christmas?" she asked Thorn once she'd settled in. She was sitting in the living room with him during their first evening at home.

"No," he said quietly, filling a glass with whiskey. "Maybe after the New Year, though, when Al and Jessica get back."

"There are only the two of us for Christmas?" she asked hesitantly.

He turned, watching her in the blue velvet robe he'd brought her. "Just the two of us," he agreed quietly.

"But, all those presents—!"

He looked uncomfortable. He sat down beside her, putting his glass to one side while he lit a cigarette. "I invited a few people over on Christmas day."

Her face went white, and his jaw tautened. "No," he said quickly. "Not anybody from that damned crowd!"

She swallowed, and clutched at her robe. She still felt vulnerable. "Sorry."

"You'll learn to trust me," he said putting

the cigarette to his mouth. "I don't make promises that I don't keep. I'll never hurt you again."

She forced a smile. "Okay."

"I invited your Mr. Rafferty and a couple of twins and their mother, and that elderly woman who lives on the first floor in your building..." he began.

Her face froze in mid-smile. "You what?"

"They're your friends, aren't they?" he said.'

"Yes! But, I never dreamed—"

"I told you I wasn't a snob," he reminded her. "I thought it was about time I proved it to you."

"But, what about your friends?" she asked, concerned.

He took the whiskey glass in his lean hand and sipped at it, laughing mirthlessly. "I don't have any."

Chapter Nine

"So you met my little community when you picked up my things at the apartment?" she asked.

"That's right," he said, turning. His eyes swept over her thin body in the deep blue velour robe. The robe was one of hers, old and worn, and his face hardened as he saw the worn places. "I looked for nightclothes, but that robe and a couple of cotton gowns were all I could find," he added.

She lowered her eyes, embarrassed. "They're all I have," she confessed. "I had to spend most of my money on stage costumes."

"You mean 'what was left.' After all, you

gave away most of what you had to your neighbors," he said.

She looked up and saw a surprising look on his face, which she was helpless to decipher. "You saw how they live," she faltered.

"Yes." He lifted the whiskey glass to his mouth and took a sip. His broad shoulders rose and fell with a heavy breath. "I suppose I've had money myself for so long that I'd forgotten what it was like to be without it." He dropped down beside her. "Not that I ever lived the way your neighbors do. My father always made good money."

She curled her feet up under her and leaned her head back against the sofa, watching him. He was good to look at, she mused. So handsome and big and vibrantly male. She smiled softly. All the bad memories faded as her heart fed on him.

He glanced at her and saw that searching look, and smiled back gently. "Feeling better?"

She nodded. "Will I have to go all the way to New York to have the stitches out?" she asked, voicing a question that had worried her for two days.

"Of course not," he said, "I've had my doctor call yours, and I've made an appointment for you on Friday. I'll drive you in to Beaumont."

"What will they do to me, do you know?" she asked, frowning.

He reached out and touched her hair lightly, tracing its sheen to her shoulder. "Just an office checkup, that's all. They'd never have let you out of the hospital if they'd had any doubts about your recovery."

"Of course." She lifted her shoulders and winced as the bruised one protested.

"How does it feel?" he asked, nodding toward her arm.

"Sore." She laughed.

He put down his whiskey glass and moved closer, opening her robe with such deft assurance that she didn't think to protest the intimacy. The gown underneath covered her of course, but it was old and worn thin. When he drew the robe away from her body, he smiled wickedly at the flush on her cheeks.

"You can't possibly be self-conscious with me?" he teased. "Not after that day in the woods."

Her eyes widened, as they looked into his, and the smile on his face began to fade. His long fingers drew a pattern down her throat, tracing the madly throbbing pulse, lingering just below her collarbone where the loose gown had sagged.

"I wanted you," he breathed. "Never more than that day, when you let me open your blouse and look at you, and touch you, and taste you." His jaw tautened as he sighed wearily. "I was so wrong about you, Sabina. I knew it then, but things had gone too far. I was afraid of what was happening to me. I hated you for leading me on, when you belonged to Al, for keeping us both on a string. I couldn't be sure you weren't the gold digger I thought you were. I didn't trust my instincts. It never occurred to me that you could have been pretending. But it should have. Everything was wrong about that engagement. A blind man could have seen through it."

"You were trying to protect Al. I realized that, although it didn't help a lot at the time," she said quietly. "I've been so ashamed of my past, you see."

"Why?" He brushed the dark hair away

from her face. "None of it was any of your doing. Your mother did what she could for you. I can see that it would have left scars, but it was never your fault."

Her eyes fell to his chest. "I was there the night my mother died—" she closed her eyes "—that last night, when he hit her..." Her voice broke.

"Darling, don't." He pulled her gently into his arms and held her and rocked her, his hand smoothing her long hair, his deep voice soothing her. "It all happened a long time ago. It's over."

She dabbed at the tears, shifting and moaning as her shoulder began to ache again.

"Did I hurt you?" he asked softly. His hand moved to her face and touched it hesitantly, learning every soft contour, as hers had once done to his, delighting in its vulnerability.

"Thorn," she whispered.

His breath became audible. His mouth was poised just above hers and his eyes looked deep into her own as his fingers passed slowly down her throat to her collarbone and still further. She tensed, but he shook his head.

"No," he whispered. "Let me touch you."

She bit her lower lip as his lean hand eased under the fabric, and he watched her as the tips of his fingers teased softly around the edges of one perfect, creamy breast.

He moved, easing her down onto the couch, and she heard the springs shift under them. But what he was doing was so delicious that she didn't even protest. She trembled with sweet anticipation, wanting him so much that it was almost painful. His arm made a pillow behind her head, and he smiled softly as her body jerked toward his fingers.

"Wicked, wicked...man," she whispered brokenly, watching his face.

"Indulge me," he whispered back. "You can't know how it was, seeing you in that hospital bed."

It was hard to think. "The nurse said...that you talked to me and...held my hand...oh!" she gasped as one lean finger brushed the hard tip of her breast.

"Did she tell you that I sat by you when they told me you might not come out of the coma, and that I cried like a boy?" He put his hard mouth slowly, warmly on hers. "Because I did. Open your mouth."

"Cried…?" She couldn't think. His tongue was working sorcery on her parted lips, and his hand had eased down completely over her bare breast, so that she could feel not only his slightly calloused fingers, but also the wrinkly moist warmth of his palm. "Thorn," she moaned, and her body arched.

"Open my shirt, and do that to me," he whispered into her mouth. "Let me teach you how to arouse me."

Her breathing became short. Her hands shook so much she could hardly fumble the buttons of his shirt open. To be allowed free license with his body was overwhelming.

She eased her fingers down against the thick mass of hair and over the warm muscles. She searched for his skin, finding taut peaks that might have been the mirror image of her own. Her eyes found his.

"Do men…too?" she whispered.

"Yes." He held her head gently in his hands. "Open your mouth, and put it against me, there," he whispered, guiding her down his chest. She did as he told her, and he groaned harshly, a sound that made her head lift so that she could see his face.

"Don't you moan when I put my lips on you?" he whispered, smiling.

Her eyes were full of wonder. "Oh, Thorn, I never knew—!"

"Thank God." He moved, peeling the gown to her waist, and she let him, lying pliant in his arms, watching his face as he saw what his stroking had accomplished. "I like knowing that you're a virgin," he said unexpectedly, touching her lightly. "You aren't afraid of the first time with me, are you?" he asked quietly.

Her face reddened. "I can't…"

"Not now, little tulip," he said with a laugh. He bent and eased his bare chest down over hers, and smiled at the way she trembled. "Yes, I like that, too. I like the way it feels to have you half nude against me. You're a sexy woman."

"Thorn, I won't be—" she tried again.

"Where would you like to be married?" he asked.

She stared at him as if he'd gone crazy. "What?"

"Where would you like to be married?" he murmured against her mouth. "Beaumont or

New Orleans? Mr. Rafferty can give you away, and Jessica can be matron of honor.''

Her palms flattened against his chest. ''I can't marry you,'' she said.

His face went expressionless. ''Why not?'' he said.

She drew a breath and tried to get up. Surprisingly, he let her, watching as she drew her gown back up and shouldered gingerly into her robe again. ''I just can't, that's all.''

''Is it your career?'' he persisted. ''Because I'll compromise.''

She shook her head. She wrapped her arms around her waist, dying inside because he'd just said the one thing she wanted most in the world to hear. She loved him, would have died for him. But she couldn't marry him.

''Then why?''

''How would you announce it?'' she asked with a bitter laugh, and ran an unsteady hand through her hair. ''My parents were never married, you know. There was a front-page story when my mother was killed. Inevitably, people would find out. In the circles you move in, I'd be so much of a liability—''

''Liability, hell! That's no excuse at all.'' He

sighed wearily and got to his feet. "It's because of what I did to you, isn't it?" he asked in an odd voice. He wouldn't look at her. He lit another cigarette, took a few draws and, as quickly, put it out. "It's because I humiliated you. You think I might do it again."

"No!" Her head came up. "No, it isn't that, truly it isn't! It's just that you'd—oh, Thorn, you'd be so ashamed of me."

His eyes closed. "The only person I've been ashamed of in recent weeks is myself." He moved restlessly toward the door. "I need to do some paperwork, I'll see you later."

She stared at his broad back, half puzzled, half certain. Did he care? Could he care that much and still not believe her reasons for rejecting his proposal? Her heart raced wildly.

She took a gamble, the maddest gamble she'd ever taken in her life. If he rejected her, she'd never get over it.

"Thorn!" she called.

He paused with his hand on the doorknob. "Yes?"

She gathered all her courage and held out both her arms to him.

He hesitated for an instant, and her heart began to throb. She feared that she'd misread the entire situation. Then his face changed. He moved back toward the sofa and suddenly dropped to his knees and clasped her hard enough around the waist to hurt her, burying his face in her breasts.

She held him, feeling the tremor in his body, her hands tangling in his dark hair. She sat disbelieving, trembling with new emotions, with shared emotions.

"I love you," he managed in a broken tone. "Oh, God, I love you, and I didn't know it until that night, until it was too late, and I wondered how I was going to live if I'd caused you to do something desperate. I called to make sure Jessica was with you because I was afraid. After that, I could never get close to you again. I knew I'd lost you, I knew I had…" His arms tightened and he caught a savage breath, while Sabina stared down at his dark head in shocked delight. "I kept up with you, I followed your career, I even paid for that damn video," he added, stunning her. "But nothing compensated me for you. I haven't been near another woman since you left. I've hardly eaten or slept…and then that damned light fell on you, and I paid for sins I haven't even committed yet. I sat by your bed and held your hand and knew that, if you died, I might as well lie down beside you, because I wouldn't have had a reason left to stay alive myself.''

"Oh, Thorn," she whispered, pulling his head closer. "I love you so much...."

His head lifted, his eyes unusually bright. "Do you? Even after all I've done to you?"

Her fingers touched his face wonderingly. "I understood even then, you know," she whispered. "I knew you so well. It frightened me sometimes, especially when I was pretending to be engaged to Al, because you were like the other half of my soul. I even knew what you were thinking."

"Yes, I felt that," he sighed. "At the church, when you said I never let people come close, you hit a nerve, darling. I hated having you know that, hated being so vulnerable, so readable. If it's any kind of compensation, I've paid for what I did to you. Being without you was more than enough punishment."

She bent down and kissed his mouth tenderly. "I want a child with you."

His breath held, and his eyes were gloriously

loving. "I want one with you. I did even that first day you came to the ranch. You mentioned having babies, and I looked at you and wanted to see you big with mine. It scared the hell out of me," he said with a chuckle. "After that, all I could think about was getting you pregnant. That was when I realized how committed I was." His smile faded. "Marry me, Sabina."

"There'll be gossip," she cautioned.

"Darling, there'll always be gossip. I love you. What else matters?"

"You're hard to argue with," she murmured.

"So they tell me." He kissed her gently. "Marry me. Give me some children. I'll buy you a new bathrobe and let you sing in my nightclub."

She laughed at his phrasing. "How can I sing when I'm pregnant?"

"Listen, lady, you can even sing while you're getting pregnant, for all I care."

"Thank you," she murmured demurely, batting her eyelashes at him. "Thorn, I hear that new vocalist is doing great with the band. And if you'd let me study opera in my spare time, and let me teach voice…"

He looked shocked. "What are you offering to do?" he asked. "Give up everything you've ever worked for?"

She slid down onto the floor in front of him and linked her arms around his neck. "I have everything I ever wanted right here," she said solemnly. "There is nothing I want more than you, and that includes a career. Later, when the children are older, perhaps. But being on the road was already beginning to pale, and I'm terrified of large crowds. I want to live with you and travel with you. I love you."

"Darling," he breathed, searching for words.

"Shhh," she whispered, putting her mouth against his. "Lie down, darling," she murmured wickedly.

"Like hell." He chuckled. He got up, smoothing his hair. "You're not getting me into bed without a wedding ring."

"Tease," she said accusingly.

He made a mock bow and helped her to her feet. "We'll set a wedding date. Meanwhile, don't you want to know who all those presents are for?"

She stared past him at the tree. "Who?"

"I got Mr.Rafferty a warm coat, and the twins some new shoes, and their mother a coat...."

Tears welled up in her eyes. "My friends...."

"The whole world is your friend," he whispered. "But I'm your best one. Between us, we'll spread a little comfort, okay?"

She reached up and pressed a warm kiss against his chin, her eyes brimming with love. "Okay."

He smiled at her. In his eyes, she saw the sweetness and laughter of the years ahead. And she laughed, softly, wonderingly, just before he lifted her in his arms and carried her back to the sofa.

"I thought you weren't going to let me get you into bed until we were married," she chided.

"I didn't say one word about sofas, did I?" he murmured with a roguish smile. He put her down on the couch and let his eyes wander slowly from her toes up over her legs and hips to her taut breasts. His hand went to the buttoned cuffs of his shirt and he flicked the buttons out of the holes with deliberate slowness while she looked up at him, lips parted, body aching.

"The door's open," she whispered.

"For your sake, we'd better leave it that way," he murmured. His lips curved in a smile. "On second thought, to hell with it." He closed the door without looking out, locked it, and went slowly back to the couch. "Now," he said in a breathless, laughing tone. "Aren't you too hot, with all those clothes on?" he murmured, easing down beside her. "Hmmmm, your skin's hot, darling," he taunted, watching her as he lazily disposed of the robe and put it aside. His mischievous eyes went down to the taut outline of her breasts, which were moving with the torturous raggedness of her breathing.

"Thorn," she whispered in a tone that throbbed with hunger.

"I want you, too," he said in a whisper. "But I'll stop before we go too far. Lift up, darling, and let me get this gown out of my way.... Yes, yes!"

Old Juan, who'd been on his way to tell them dinner was ready, had watched the door close and simultaneously turned around on his heel, smiling, to go back to the kitchen. Time enough to eat, he told himself. There were more important things. He put the plates aside and began to hum.

Take 2 of "The Best of the Best™" Novels FREE

Plus get a FREE surprise gift!

Special Limited-Time Offer

Mail to The Best of the Best™

3010 Walden Avenue
P.O. Box 1867
Buffalo, N.Y. 14240-1867

YES! Please send me 2 free novels and my free surprise gift. Then send me 3 of "The Best of the Best™" novels each month. I'll receive the best books by the world's hottest romance authors. Bill me at the low price of $4.24 each plus 25¢ delivery per book and applicable sales tax, if any.* That's the complete price, and a saving of over 20% off the cover prices—quite a bargain! I understand that accepting the books and gift places me under no obligation ever to buy any books. I can always return a shipment and cancel at any time. Even if I never buy another book, the 2 free books and the surprise gift are mine to keep forever.

183 MEN CH74

Name	(PLEASE PRINT)	
Address	Apt. No.	
City	State	Zip

This offer is limited to one order per household and not valid to current subscribers.
*Terms and prices are subject to change without notice. Sales tax applicable in N.Y.
All orders subject to approval.

UBOB-98